Elaine's Unwanted Choice

Sarah Lamb

This is a work of fiction. Names, characters, businesses, places, events, locales, and incidents are either the products of the author's imagination or used in a fictitious manner. Any resemblance to actual persons, living or dead, or actual events is purely coincidental.

A thank you to my proofreader, Brooke, and all of the lovely women who help ARC read to catch those typos I miss!

This book was not written by AI. Any typos are proudly (and embarrassingly!) my own human created ones!

Paperback ISBN: 978-1-960418-69-2

Large print ISBN: 978-1-960418-70-8

Contents

V

1. Chapter 1 — 1
2. Chapter 2 — 11
3. Chapter 3 — 19
4. Chapter 4 — 29
5. Chapter 5 — 35
6. Chapter 6 — 41
7. Chapter 7 — 51
8. Chapter 8 — 61
9. Chapter 9 — 71
10. Chapter 10 — 79
11. Chapter 11 — 85

12. Chapter 12 93
13. Chapter 13 103
14. Chapter 14 111
15. Chapter 15 119
16. Chapter 16 127
17. Chapter 17 135
18. Chapter 18 141
19. Chapter 19 151
20. Chapter 20 159
21. Epilogue 167
22. Note from Author 171
23. Want more Rejected Books or those set in Cottonwood Falls? 173
24. About the Author 180

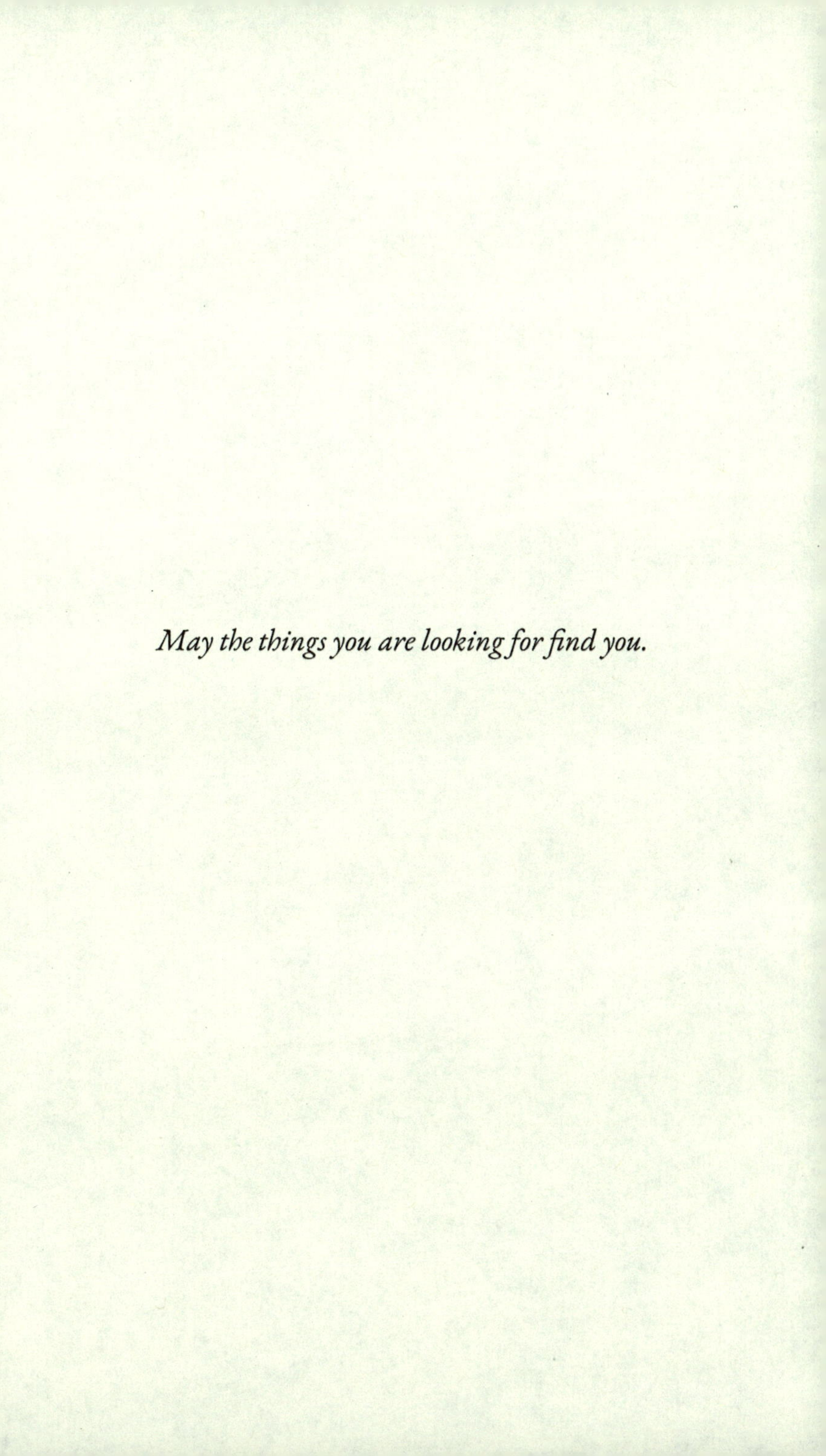

May the things you are looking for find you.

Chapter 1

Kansas, 1881

The smell of the soup—watery though it was—made Elaine Winters's stomach growl. As she watched it simmer in the battered cooking pot, she felt relief that tonight her stomach would be full.

It had been another long day of searching for work. How was it no one in the town was hiring for more than an odd job or two? Worse, that it had been that way for nearly six months! Luckily, today she'd been hired to tend a young widow's garden. The woman hadn't had coin to pay her, but offered her a few potatoes and carrots and an onion. The contents of this blessed meal.

Elaine had taken it, because what other choice did she have? Pride didn't fill an empty belly. The small wheat loaf her friend and roommate Lizzie had made two days before was gone, and they'd had nothing to eat today. Their situation was getting desperate.

Elaine's fingers curled around the locket at her neck, her finger finding the small hollow she always reached for. It was all she had of any value, but she'd rather starve before selling the only thing she had of her mother's.

"Maybe Lizzie had a better day seeking work than I did," Elaine said, the words and desperate hope escaping as she returned to the task at hand and stirred the bubbling pot.

As if she'd summoned her friend, Lizzie entered the kitchen of the barely standing house they shared with a handful of other people, all in various stages of their struggles.

"You will not believe what happened," Lizzie said, coming over to the pot where she sniffed the soup appreciatively.

"I hope it's good news," Elaine said. "We could use some."

"It is," Lizzie said, her face lit up. Then it fell slightly. She twirled a long, dark strand of hair nervously. "At least, it is for me. I'm sorry. I just realized that my good news will make your life more difficult."

Elaine raised a brow. "We are friends, and whatever wonderful thing has happened to you, I will be happy for. Never you mind about me. I've always managed to take care of myself."

And it was true. Elaine hadn't had things easy. She'd been left as an infant on the doorstep of an orphanage, with only a note saying *Elaine* and the half locket wrapped around her throat. She didn't know for sure, but Elaine liked to imagine it belonged to her mother, a woman who had loved her, but had no choice but to leave her.

She had stayed at the orphanage until she was sixteen, and then left, a young woman seeking a brighter future. Between the education she was given and her last name, she'd always carried a piece of the school with her. It was the head of the school who'd given her the last name Winters, because it was wintertime when she was found.

Upon leaving the orphanage, she'd been fortunate enough to be hired as a maid for a hotel where she had worked until the building had burned down six months ago. Since then, she'd struggled to find more work, and now, at age twenty-four, she was desperate for a little bit more to life than struggle.

Was that why her mother had left her? She, too, was struggling, perhaps a widow, and had wished for a better life for her babe? Elaine hoped so. The alternatives—her mother having died or too selfish to want her—were heartbreaking, and she never let herself think those.

Elaine didn't mind hard work. She'd grown up with it. It was just the uncertainty of what she would now do that ate at her. She liked routines and stability. Knowing what would happen each day. The last six months had been anything but steady or with a schedule for her day. Unless one counted hours of walking, and going door to door seeking employment.

Which was why Lizzie's news must be celebrated.

"Out with it," Elaine ordered, filling their bowls. A lovely bit of orange carrot floated to the top of one, and her mouth watered. She reached for two spoons. "I want to hear."

Lizzie nodded, and sat at the rickety table on a three-legged stool. "Well, I was offered a job." She pulled a bowl toward her.

"That's wonderful!" Elaine said. "Where?"

The expression on her friend's face wavered. "It's...it's as a lady's traveling companion. So, I will be going to quite a few places. We'll make our way to New York where we will stay for a month before we set sail for England and France. She specifically wanted someone who could speak French and braid hair, and I met just what she was looking for."

It took a moment, but the words *traveling companion* finally sank in. Lizzie would be leaving. For just a moment, Elaine felt sorrow. She loved Lizzie like a sister, and would miss her dearly. When she returned—if she returned—would things ever be the same between them? Or would Lizzie be too sophisticated to spend time with someone such as Elaine was?

Elaine forced a breath into her tight chest and a smile onto her face. “How exciting,” she said. “You've always wanted to see the world.”

“I have,” Lizzie said quietly. “But what will you do, Elaine? We split the cost of our rent for the room we share.”

“Oh, I'll just find someone else,” Elaine answered far more cheerfully than she felt. “Or else I will simply have my turn at finding a job and won't need to worry about it. I am due any day, you know.”

Her friend's troubled eyes turned downward into her soup. “I can pay this week,” Lizzie said softly. “And next. Next is when I start. But it might help buy you a little more time.”

Elaine nodded, unable to speak around the lump in her throat.

“Maybe she wants a second maid,” Lizzie said, hope in her voice as she looked up. “She's already got one. As her companion, I'll just keep her entertained and help with her hair sometimes. Rich women always love to have lots of maids.”

“Can you imagine me as a lady's maid?” Elaine laughed, and it was genuine. “Oh, I wouldn't know the first thing about fancy dresses or hairstyles! And you know I can't speak anything but English. Well, perhaps Dog Latin.”

“Oh dear,” Lizzie said with a laugh of her own. “Can you imagine a fancy woman hearing you talk that way? You are right. Mrs. Middleton wouldn't be pleased. She seems a fussy sort."

"And you are content with working for such a woman?" Elaine asked. "More than that, having to amuse her if needed?"

Her friend shrugged. "I don't mind. I'll get to see places I've only read about in books. And, I'll be able to get references to find another job one day if I want. She plans to travel for a year, and afterward, I don't know what will happen to me. References will be important."

"You will figure it out," Elaine assured her. "But, with any luck, she will travel for years and you will enjoy each moment. Or, when she returns, she'll be so fond of you, she won't want you to leave. I will miss you," Elaine told her. "So, be sure you write."

"I will," Lizzie promised. Then she gasped. "Oh! That reminds me!"

"Of what?" Elaine asked, dividing the last of the soup between them, shaking every drop from the pot.

Lizzie dug through her handbag. "I forgot all about it until just now. I had a letter."

"Goodness! What a day for you. Anything interesting?" Elaine asked.

"I don't know," her friend said, loosening the seal. "I can't think who it's from."

Elaine tried not to feel envious. First, Lizzie got a job. Then a letter. She wished something good would happen to her. It had seemed to her that other than meeting Lizzie at the hotel, and the job there, her life had been a series of unfortunate events, and she was drifting along like a tumbleweed, trying to find her way to the place where she could stay and build a life.

But just as soon as the thought came, Elaine pushed it aside. It wasn't right to feel selfish. She was happy for her friend, Elaine reminded herself. As she should be. She shouldn't let her insecurities cloud that and make her feel bitter or jealous. Happy news—even if it was not her own—was welcome. Lizzie had her own difficulties and deserved to have good things as well. She—

"This is it!" Lizzie gasped, and shook the letter, thrusting it toward Elaine.

Elaine's brows furrowed and she shook her head. She couldn't make out the letter from this distance, especially with Lizzie shaking it about. "What's it?"

"The answer to your problem." Lizzie grinned, and stopped waving her hand around.

"Is it a job offer?" Elaine asked eagerly, leaning forward to see better.

"Well, sort of. Do you remember about six months ago, just before the hotel burned down, I had applied for a mail-order bride position at the Marston Mail-Order Bride Agency?"

Elaine searched her memories, then nodded. "I think so. That was when we both had good jobs and lived at the hotel and you were getting rather tired of your job. But you hadn't heard back, as I recall."

"Not until now. It seems my letter to them got delayed, but they have a potential husband."

"But what about your new job?" Elaine asked. "As the lady's companion. I don't think she'd approve of you bringing some man along."

Her friend rolled her eyes. "Not for me, silly. That's why I said it was the answer to your problem. You should take my place!"

"Me," Elaine answered flatly.

"Yes. They won't know you aren't me. The man won't care. He just wants a wife." Lizzie shook the letter again. "It's perfect."

"Except for one thing," Elaine told her friend, dryly. "I'd like to have some say in who I marry. It's rather a unique idea, I know, but that's how I feel. While yes, things are desperate, are they marriage desperate? I'm not sure."

"You have complete say," Lizzie assured her. "Listen." She cleared her throat and read, "'If you find the gentleman not to your liking, we will present you with other options.' See? It's *fool*proof."

"Or *fool*ish," Elaine said.

Lizzie scowled. "I'm trying to help. Why must you be stubborn? You've been looking for work and there isn't anything around here. This might be the perfect thing for you. He might be rich, good looking, kind. I don't know."

Elaine bit her lip. “Or he might be awful. We know nothing about him!”

“In which case, you write the agency and tell them so. There are travel funds enclosed. And a stage ticket.”

She pushed the ticket to Elaine, who read from it, “Cottonwood Falls, Kansas.”

“It sounds nice,” Lizzie said, her voice hopeful. “Doesn’t it?”

Elaine nodded, but she knew firsthand how names could be deceiving. After all, the orphanage had called itself Sunshine Acres, and most days the place had been as gloomy as midnight in a storm.

“At least think on it,” Lizzie pleaded. “It might be a good opportunity.”

As her friend looked at her hopefully, Elaine felt herself tense. Part of her wanted what the letter promised. Not just a husband, but a home. A place to belong. But how could a stranger offer that? The other part of her was far too practical to think that help would come in the offer of marriage to someone she didn’t know.

“I will,” Elaine finally said. “But I’m not sure yet.”

“That is all I ask,” her friend said.

Lizzie returned the letter and its contents to her handbag and continued chattering about the letter and her job, but Elaine had stopped listening. Not because she didn’t care, but because there was a niggling worry that filled her head at the thought of going, and it wasn’t just her preference for knowing what to expect, and some sort of order and predictability.

No, it was that tiny voice inside warning her that doing this might be a very, very big mistake.

Chapter 2

Cottonwood Falls, Kansas

Through the open window, the sounds of Cottonwood Falls trickled into Oliver's ears. He enjoyed how very different they were, when compared to where he had grown up in the bustling town of Boston, Massachusetts.

There, the streets were packed with people, many of whom stood on corners and shouted about their wares. Everything from newspapers and fruit to rodent hunting or mending of all kinds. It was always noisy, and the streets were filled with sludge from the endless stream of horses pulling carriages, which led to a rank smell that never fully dissipated, kept close by the buildings that seemed to cover every square inch of the town.

In contrast, Cottonwood Falls was filled with wide open spaces, fresh air that swept through the town smelling faintly of wildflowers and sweet hay, and entirely different sounds. There was the slow plodding of horse hooves pulling a creaking wagon, the blacksmith's hammer faintly banging in rhythm, the distant sound of children happily playing in the schoolyard. When he squinted, he could even see a few dots far out that were horses and cattle.

It was a nice change, and Oliver had discovered that though he had only been here two weeks, he enjoyed each moment of the place. With enough luck, he'd be able to make the town his permanent home.

Still, Oliver couldn't help but worry. Though he was happy to be here, not everyone was happy he'd come. And, if Melanie—

A knock at his door broke him from his thoughts, and Oliver hurried from his study to the front door.

As he opened it, a grinning face met his. "Cousin!"

Oliver's smile matched that of the one worn by his cousin, Dr. Edward Mason. "Come in!" he invited, clasping his cousin's arm. "Back from your trip, I see."

"Yes, and my backside and legs are grateful," Edward answered. "Traveling by stage isn't the most comfortable."

"Perhaps one day the train will come through," Oliver said. "Though, I'm not sure I'd want the noise of it."

"My feelings are the same." Edward followed him into his study, then handed him a set of slim brown books. "These are my financial ledgers," he said. "Have I told you how glad I am that you've moved here to do accounting?"

"Only a few times," Oliver teased. "But forgetfulness happens in one's advanced years."

His cousin barked out a laugh, then said, "I am not old yet! But what a help this will be! While I've managed on my own for a good number of years, it takes more time that I could be using to help my patients. As the town grows, so do the number of patients I see. Even with Caroline tending a good many of them, it feels like I always have more to do than time."

"They will be in good hands," Oliver promised. "As your patients are in your hands and hers."

Edward had been quite fortunate in meeting Caroline. Not only did he love her dearly, but she was also very competent medically. She'd started off as his nurse, and then became a doctor herself.

Oliver pulled out his pocket watch and checked the time. "Are you free for lunch?"

"I'm afraid I've got to drive out to a few patients," Edward said regretfully. "Does tomorrow work for you?"

"It does indeed," Oliver said. "At whatever time suits you. Right now, I have very little on my schedule."

"Excellent." Edward patted the ledgers, then strode toward the front door. "I will be here shortly before noon."

"Tell Caroline and the little one I said hello," Oliver called as his cousin went into the street, and then closed the door behind him.

He returned to his study, where he unwrapped a small package that had arrived earlier that morning. The time had come to place it. With a grin, he studied the plaque and read, "Oliver Mason, Accountant."

The sign filled him with pride, and the feeling only grew as he carefully hung it upon the nail near the front door and then straightened it.

But as he admired it, that pride suddenly soured. He felt doubt. Fear. What if he wasn't ready? Here, on his own, without anyone to seek accounting advice from if he got into his head.

Oliver shook his head, trying to chase the negative thoughts away. Of course he was ready! This would be no different from what he'd been doing back East. There, he worked for someone else, and here, he was his own boss.

He could do this. Had to.

Hopefully, the sign, along with his visiting the local businesses, would lead to more work. He only had three clients just now, Edward, the mill owner, and the town lawyer, but he was sure that more would follow, especially once he was fully situated as a member of the community. Things took time. And Oliver was nothing but patient. He had to be in this profession. One small mistake might make an enormous difference when it came to numbers.

Yet, there was that feeling of impatience, to grow his business. Oliver wanted to have a good number of clients before his fiancée arrived. Melanie was accustomed to a particular way of life, and as of this moment, he wouldn't be able to provide it. Not with only three clients. Though he'd saved for a year of expenses before starting this endeavor, Oliver was feeling a little nervous things might not work out.

Which was why he should never have left Boston, he could almost hear his father saying. No matter that he needed to. That he felt as though he were suffocating in the city, being smothered by the business and the social events and the expectations others had for him. Though he'd have had many contacts and more business than he could have managed, he hadn't wanted to work there or live there.

Truthfully, Oliver also hadn't wanted to get married. It was not something he'd planned to do for quite some time. However, both his father and hers had told him that it would lend legitimacy to his fledgling business. Oliver could remember the night he asked her. Melanie's eyes had been wide, hesitant. Her face startled. Then, her parents had walked in, very excited to see the proposal, and she'd said yes.

Had she really wanted to? She'd seemed delighted, but that had faded once she realized that he hadn't planned to stay there in their hometown, but move here, to the middle of nowhere, as she'd declared it more than once.

By that point, they couldn't call the wedding off. It would have made him look bad and upset Melanie and their families since the announcement had been in the papers and had traveled around social circles. Their joining in matrimony wasn't about love, but appearances. Though they'd been friends for a long time, having grown up together, he wasn't sure friendship would blossom into love, or how happy she'd be when she came here.

He also had the feeling that she'd be trying her hardest to get him to hang his new plaque up back in Boston. A woman like Melanie wouldn't be happy in such a small town. She was used to being with her friends, enjoying afternoon teas and beautiful garden parties. He could almost see her wide eyes, her slightly turned-up nose, and imagine her handkerchief held to her nose when someone rode through town and kicked up dust. And how restless she would be without the entertainments she was used to.

Oliver loved this town and wanted to make it his own. More than anything, he wanted the chance to prove to himself and to others that he was capable of running his own business. Even if it took time to grow. He could be patient. The problem was, could she?

His father's voice echoed. *You'll never make it on your own, boy. Melanie needs a man to provide for her. Stay here, where you'll be something.*

Though his father had meant well, the words had been painful to hear, and each time they went around in his mind, he struggled more. Yes, he knew Melanie needed to be provided for. That's why he was here, wasn't it? To build his business. Make something of himself.

Melanie would understand it took time. Wouldn't she? Her lovely face flashed through his mind, but it was the disappointment on it that made his heart ache and his stomach sink. He didn't want to disappoint her. That wasn't his intention in coming here.

He picked up the letter that had arrived from her yesterday, with the request for a housekeeper. It wasn't an unreasonable request, not really. She was used to one and a cook and several maids. He just wasn't sure where he could find a housekeeper. He'd have to make inquiries. Perhaps Edward would know of someone. Tomorrow at lunch he'd ask.

It would be good for him as well, having someone to take care of meals and the management of his house, allowing him to do the work he needed to do. With any luck, he'd be able to find her before Melanie arrived, so that she could help prepare things.

Oliver dropped Melanie's letter into his desk drawer and closed it. Perhaps he was worried about nothing and was being critical without reason. Maybe Melanie was just nervous about their upcoming wedding, and moving away from all she'd known and grown up with. He could understand that.

There was also the fact that they'd never really been romantically interested in each other. Neither of them had ever entertained the idea. Until that day. Everything felt arranged. Life changing. Not everyone looked forward to change, and he sometimes forgot that.

While he was embracing this new chapter in life here in Cottonwood Falls—or trying to, anyway—she might not be ready. But that didn't mean he should be so cynical. Many a successful marriage had been made based on mutual needs, necessity. Having a friendship was a great advantage. It was also more than some couples had. Surely, love would follow.

Oliver took a deep breath and then closed his eyes. He hoped that was the case, anyway. Otherwise, he had the feeling that his life was about to become quite stressful.

Chapter 3

Elaine had decided that marrying a stranger wasn't for her. She planned to tell Lizzie so and thank her for the idea, even if she was declining.

At least...that had been her plan until the fourth day when she hadn't been able to find any work, not even an odd job that paid in food. In two more days, rent was due and she didn't have her share. She was also so hungry that she was feeling lightheaded.

Feet aching from walking through the town and the outskirts all day in her worn shoes, she nearly limped back home. As she walked inside, the smell of someone having baked bread made her stomach grumble, but she ignored it, intending to go into the kitchen for a drink of warm water. That was all she could do to quell the ache. There wasn't even anything to flavor it, and nothing else had gone into her stomach for two days.

To her surprise, as she walked into the kitchen, Lizzie was the one with the bread, and in the middle of slicing it. Elaine's mouth watered as she looked at her friend in surprise.

"It's my last night here," Lizzie said, not quite meeting her eyes, "and I thought we should eat together."

"You didn't have to," Elaine protested, even as she took the warm slice from Lizzie, breathing in deeply and savoring it before she took a small bite. The soft, yeasty taste exploded in her mouth, and Elaine was sure she'd never tasted anything so good.

"I can't very well start my new job if I waste away from hunger or I'm in mourning for my best friend who has," Lizzie said with a shrug, and a teasing look on her face. She handed Elaine another thick slice. "We will save the rest for breakfast and eat together before I leave."

Elaine nodded, and the two ate slowly. It didn't matter there was no butter or jam or cheese or anything to go with it. There would be no complaints from her.

Other than the shifting wood in the cookstove, the kitchen was quiet. Finally, Lizzie asked, "Have you thought about it?"

There was no need to ask what she meant by *it*. Lizzie hadn't pressed. In fact, she'd not even brought up the subject again, but as this was her last chance to answer, Elaine needed to reply.

"I have," Elaine said. "I had planned to say no. But now..."

Lizzie didn't answer as she slid the envelope to her. "It's worth a shot. If it doesn't work out, they'll find you someone new. Or, maybe you'll have found a job and it won't matter."

Elaine blew out a breath, squaring her shoulders. "You are right. It's not like I've any other choice, is it?"

"I'll write," Lizzie said, her voice quavering. "I don't know how often I can mail the letters, but I will."

"And I will reply," Elaine said, tears forming in her own eyes. She reached a hand up to touch her locket and took a deep breath, squeezing her fingers around the locket and trying to steady herself. "Look at us. New adventures ahead."

"A future that's going to be wonderful," Lizzie agreed, though her voice wobbled.

They sat there, neither of them saying anything more. There wasn't anything to say. They'd cried the night before, promised each other that it wasn't goodbye, but Elaine wasn't sure that was the truth. Who knew what the future held? When she arrived, she might be in just as much of a difficult situation as she was here, but it was worth a try. There was nothing more to do.

Elaine finally nodded. "Right. Well then, I'd best pack. The future awaits and I don't want to go empty-handed. You should finish as well."

Lizzie nodded, and they returned to their room. The rest of the evening was spent packing their few belongings and pretending that everything was fine. Elaine slept fitfully, and when she and Lizzie finally couldn't linger any longer over breakfast, they hugged tightly and said goodbye, Lizzie walking in one direction, Elaine in another.

It felt strange to be walking over to the stagecoach office. Elaine had never been in a stage herself, but Lizzie had, and told her that it might be cramped, and it wouldn't stop often. Elaine was prepared for both situations, but hoped that it wouldn't be the case for either.

She was relieved when there were only three other passengers for the day-long trip—a man who immediately took out a newspaper and buried himself in it, and an older couple who both fell asleep the moment the conveyance started. It was quite fine with her, and Elaine tried to occupy her frantic mind by looking through the window, watching the last of all she knew go past, but it was hard.

All the worries and fears she'd been trying to stuff down since she'd agreed to take Lizzie's mail-order marriage offer kept surfacing. She knew nothing about the man, and he would know nothing about her ahead of time.

She and Lizzie had decided she should simply pretend the mail-order agency got her name wrong. Their names were so similar anyway, surely the man wouldn't even notice. However, she had more worries than that.

Would it be a problem for him that she was an orphan? She imagined the subject would come up when they asked each other about their families, since that seemed to be a standard question when getting to know someone.

It had been difficult to get the job at the hotel because of her past. The head housekeeper had told her flat out that most orphans were thieves, and she'd be watching her closely. Would this man be suspicious of her as well?

Elaine was nothing but honest—in manner and speech. Not that everyone appreciated that. But she'd never take something that wasn't hers. Even though a good deal of time had passed, the hurtful words stayed in her mind.

"Next stop! Cottonwood Falls!" the driver roared finally. "Half hour ahead!"

The couple across from her roused, and the woman smiled, pushing back some strands of silvery hair. "That means we will be home in an hour," she told her husband. Then, her eyes fell on Elaine. "Where are you headed?"

"The next stop," Elaine said faintly.

"Someone special waiting for you?" the woman asked, nodding toward the letter Elaine had been clutching in her hand for the last hour.

"No, er, that is, I'm a...mail-order bride, and that's where he is." Elaine took a deep breath. "Hopefully, I'll find him easily enough."

"How exciting!" the woman told her. "I was one myself, quite some time ago, but we are so happy together, and I am sure that you will be as well."

Seeing the honesty in the other woman's eyes made Elaine relax slightly. Perhaps things would go better than she feared. The stage began to slow and Elaine quickly gathered her handbag, read the letter once more, and then made her way to the door.

"Good luck!" the woman called cheerily.

"Thank you!" Elaine replied, and then pointed out her bag to the driver who had climbed up to get it.

"Here you are, miss," he told her, setting it down, then climbed back into his seat.

Elaine watched as the stagecoach hurried away, and her eyes fell on a large sign welcoming her to the town.

"Cottonwood Falls. The place where dreams come true," she whispered as she read it. "I certainly hope that's true."

Elaine glanced around, and then approached who she hoped might be the stage manager. "Sir, I'm looking for a man named Harold Smith."

"Old Harry?" the man asked. "Why, that's him right there."

Her eyes followed where his finger was pointing, and her stomach lurched. Sitting on a nearby bench, her future husband was picking at his teeth. His eyes met hers and he stood.

"Well, lookie here," he said, eying her from the tip of her head to the toes of her worn boots. "You my little wife? Got news one was coming that I might like this time."

This time? What did he mean?

"I...I was sent from the Marston Mail-Order Agency, however," Elaine said, trying to sound sure of herself, "as to if we are to marry, that is yet to be decided. I thought perhaps we could get to know each other a little first before we come to our decision."

Even as she spoke the words, Elaine worried that she might not have much choice but to marry the man. While the agency had promised her another match, if this was the first one they'd chosen, what hope did she have for something better?

"What for?" the man asked. "I done told them what I wanted. A wife to cook and clean and give me sons. Also, a rich one. You talk fancy enough."

He squinted then at her worn dress and frowned. "You do got money, don't you? None of them others did, but you're pretty enough, I'm willing to overlook it if you don't. Getting tired of waiting."

Elaine was so startled, it took a moment for her to stop blinking. She shook her head. "No, I...I don't have money. And, I'm not much of a cook."

"I ain't got much teeth," he told her proudly. "So soup is fine. I'll take you. Come on. Pastor's over this way."

"Sir," Elaine said, taking a small step backward, "I don't think this is going to work."

"Now, don't you worry," he told her. "I'll make do. I ain't offering charity though. You'll work for everything you git."

"I'm not expecting charity," Elaine said, pressing her lips together in a firm line. "But I am expecting a mutually agreeable situation, and this one is not."

With a speed faster than she'd have given a man obviously a few decades older than her, he lunged forward and grabbed her wrist.

"Release me at once," Elaine gasped, trying to free herself.

"Ain't gonna," the man said. "Ordered me a wife, and that's what I'm going home with. Jest told you, tired of waiting for one. Guess you and your fancy words will have to do."

Elaine struggled to pull away, but the man half dragged her toward a small white building she assumed was the church. She frantically tried to twist around, to call for help, but the street and the stage office were both empty.

"Stop!" she ordered loudly, trying to make her voice forceful. Perhaps someone would hear her and help. "I'm not marrying you."

To her surprise, the man did stop. But a cold look came across his face, and he leaned in. His breath made her want to recoil even further. "We can do this the easy way, and you walk on over with me," he told her. "Or, we can do it the way we were, and you'll pay for it later."

Every muscle in Elaine's body tensed, and she felt a fear like she'd never experienced before. Her eyes darted through the empty streets and then back to the man in front of her, waiting for her reply.

Chapter 4

"I envy you," Oliver said quietly, as he dug his fork into the slice of cherry pie in front of him. "Everything has worked out so well for you."

"There have been moments where things aren't so rosy," his cousin said wryly. "Like when Caroline and I were kidnapped. I'm no gunslinger, you know. And there are always some struggles one must face, even if they aren't necessarily dangerous. No life is perfect, but I am content with mine, and that is all that matters."

Oliver nodded, but didn't answer. What would that feel like? He'd experienced contentment for a short time when he'd planned out his business, found the building near to Edward, and made ready to venture forth on his own. But then...

He couldn't stop the sigh that came out, and Edward asked, his serious eyes studying him carefully, "Are you nervous about your new venture? Finding clients?"

"A little." Oliver shrugged. "But not really. I know they will come once others tell them how I've made their lives easier. Bookkeeping is something that is both difficult and boring for many. I'm fortunate enough to enjoy numbers, so it makes sense I enjoy my job."

"If that isn't what's wrong, then what is bothering you?" Edward asked. "You can't deny it; I see it on your face. You've been distracted today."

"I apologize," Oliver said, dabbing at his mouth with his napkin. "Melanie is arriving soon."

"Ah! Eagerness then," Edward said with a grin, but then his eyes narrowed and he sat back slightly. "It's not, is it?"

Oliver didn't answer, but instead asked, "How did you know that Caroline was the one for you?"

A distant look came over Edward's eyes, and he finally answered, "I just knew. There was a peace that came over me when she was around, and an emptiness when she wasn't there. A moment came when I thought she might be taken from me, and I vowed afterward to myself that if she would have me, that I'd spend my life making her happy."

There was silence between them, then Edward quietly asked, "Is Melanie...is she..."

"I don't know what she is," Oliver answered. "I just know she's not that for me. We've always been friends, but I never felt more. Nor do I think she did."

"Then why are the two of you engaged?" Edward asked.

Oliver studied his cousin's face. This was something he'd always appreciated about Edward. There was no judgment on his face. Only a genuine question and, Oliver suspected, some advice waiting at the ready. It was that which he sought. Just as he had when he'd written his cousin seeking advice on opening his own business.

"I don't know," Oliver admitted. "I feel as though I was talked into it."

"Do you want to be married?" Edward asked.

"Yes, I think so. Just..." He stopped.

"Perhaps not to her?" Edward finished.

"I'm going to try," Oliver said, meaning every word. "She doesn't deserve anything but my best efforts."

"You are right," Edward agreed. "But don't you think it better for the both of you if you don't marry, if you think you aren't suited?" Before Oliver could answer, he asked, "How does Melanie feel?"

"She seemed fine with being engaged," Oliver said, frowning as he thought back to that day. "I think. However, I fear my lifestyle will not suit her." He paused, then tried to hide the hurt in his voice as he added, "She has said so many times."

"That might be a problem indeed," Edward said. "Or, it simply might be that she is also anxious herself, and perhaps acting in a way she is truly not. Without knowing her as well as you do, I can't say."

"Perhaps," Oliver said slowly.

Was that it? Perhaps he was being unfair. Before they were promised to each other, he and Melanie had enjoyed each other's company. The idea of marriage, starting a new business, moving to a new town, those were all stressors in one's life, and perhaps that was why he'd been feeling this way. It very well could be that he was simply reading far more into Melanie's words and letters than she'd intended. After all, this was new for both of them.

But the more he thought about that, how he wanted to believe it was true, the knot in his stomach suggested otherwise.

"You've made me feel better," Oliver said. "I think you might be right. Sometimes I see things in such a particular way—you have to in my line of work. With numbers, there is no room for interpretation, simply facts, and I suspect I am misreading her."

"If you think I can help in any way, just—" Edward stopped, and then tensed.

Oliver followed his gaze and then was on his feet before he realized it. As he hurried to the door, he was aware of Edward dropping money onto the table and joining him.

"Let me go! You are hurting me!" a woman cried out.

As Oliver broke into a run, he glanced around. Where was everyone? It was a small town, but the streets were not usually so empty.

Ahead, about three hundred feet, a rough-looking man had twisted the arm of a young woman, and was forcing her down the street.

"Do you know her?" Oliver asked to Edward, as they rushed toward the commotion.

"No, but I bet that's her bag in the street, and she's new to town," Edward answered. "The question is, why is that man forcing her to go with him? From this distance, I can't see who it is."

It wouldn't have mattered to Oliver if it were someone important. His attention was purely focused on the woman who was being shoved up the church steps.

They were closer now, able to gain speed as the woman dragged her feet.

"Harry Smith!" Edward called out.

The man paused, but only for a moment. It was enough, however, to give the woman an opening, and she twisted away again, kicking out at the man as he hoisted her up the stairs. There was a loud howl from Harry, and the anger on his face was evident. He dropped her, causing her to stumble, then he pulled back his arm and swung it to strike at her.

Oliver didn't know how he did it, but suddenly, he was there, the other man's fist caught in his hand, a mere breath away from her face. The woman cowered before him, her eyes darting between him and Harry Smith.

Chapter 5

As Elaine struggled, trying to get away from the man she'd been sent to marry, she didn't care if she made a spectacle. She would not be marrying him, no matter what he said. Surely, no pastor would force her!

But as soon as she thought that, she remembered the empty streets, the unanswered cries for help, and realized she might be entirely on her own to get herself to safety. What if this were one of those towns ruled by fear and criminals? The pastor might be the same. She'd have no choice. She simply must escape.

With a grunt, the man grabbed her waist and started to heft her up the stairs. She twisted and cried out as best she could through the pain of his arms digging into her sides, which made her nearly breathless. The singular thought that raced through her mind was she wished she had never come.

Someone called out, but her pain-addled mind couldn't quite grasp the words. A spot of movement came from her left. Two men were rushing toward them. He must have accomplices! Elaine struggled against Mr. Smith, trying with all her might to break free. One of her boots struck his leg and he howled, then dropped her.

Seizing the moment, Elaine tried to scramble away, but Mr. Smith was there, and everything seemed to happen in slow motion. His fist came toward her face, and she knew without a doubt that it would hit her. There was nowhere to go.

But then something blocked it. A man stood between her and Mr. Smith, and his face was one of thunder. She blinked, trying to understand what was happening, while her heart beat with terror. Elaine looked between the two men who'd now arrived and Mr. Smith. She was too frightened to speak. Were they going to force her into the church? Was one the pastor?

There was now a crowd around them, but she couldn't see Mr. Smith. She just knew he wasn't there, but the two men who'd been rushing toward him were. Elaine glanced around fearfully, backing away. "Don't hurt me, please," she begged.

The man who'd come between her and Mr. Smith stepped closer. "I won't. I promise. I'm here to help you. Are you hurt?" His voice was warm, steady, grounding.

For an instant, she looked up at him to see dark hair, a handsome face, and someone a little taller than she was. She shook her head as her eyes darted away. Even if she had been, she wouldn't have said so. She couldn't let herself show any weakness. Who knew how they'd take advantage of it? Better they think she was fine, than almost about to fall over because her legs were shaking so much.

The second man she'd seen moved closer. "Miss, I'm Dr. Edward Mason. This is my cousin Oliver Mason. We aren't going to harm you, but I'd like to make sure you are all right."

A doctor. She was safe. Elaine felt some of the tension ease as she glanced around. Her gaze fell to another man, who'd just run up. He wore a sheriff's star pinned to him and added, "And find out what happened."

She took a deep breath. It was a relief to see so many people now, and that Mr. Smith was nowhere in sight, but it was also unsettling. What would happen once they left? Would he come after her again? The man's terrible promise about what would happen to her made her feel sick to her stomach, though she tried not to show it.

"Shall we go inside?" the doctor asked, gesturing to the church. "Sit for a little?"

"No." Elaine shook her head. "I won't marry him."

"You won't be forced to do anything," Mr. Mason told her.

She looked into his eyes briefly, then looked away again nervously. He seemed to be speaking the truth, but Elaine didn't want to take a chance that he wasn't. Not after all that had happened. She'd never known a man to be kind unless he wanted something from her.

"Now what's all this?" an older woman asked, stepping forward, hands on her hips.

"Mrs. Harper," the doctor said with a polite nod. "I'm not quite sure."

The woman gave Elaine a quick look, and said, "New to town?"

"Yes, ma'am," Elaine said. "I am—was—a mail-order bride. But I thought I had the right to say I didn't wish to marry. My letter said so." She fumbled around looking for her belongings. "My bags!" she gasped.

"I'll get them," Mr. Mason offered, and ran off toward her bag and reticule that were in the street. When he returned, she took them with a thank-you. As their fingers brushed, she found herself surprised at the warmth in them, mirrored by that in his eyes.

Some of the fear she'd felt had dissipated. It helped, Mrs. Harper being there. Elaine sensed the woman's kindness and didn't feel quite so alone. Perhaps not everyone in town was as dreadful as Mr. Smith.

"I had a letter. It said that I didn't have to marry," she repeated, her voice strained as she produced it, as though it would provide the answers to what she should do next. And what was she to do? She had no idea.

"You don't need to do anything you don't want, dear," Mrs. Harper said. "I run the boardinghouse. You come stay with me until you get things figured out. What's your name?"

"Elaine," she said. "I'd be grateful, but..." she drew in a deep breath and admitted, "I have no money. I—I am a hard worker, though. Would you let me trade labor for a room? Just while I figure out what to do and seek a temporary job?"

The boarding house owner nodded. "Let's work out the details. My place isn't far. You can tell me everything that's happened and perhaps I can make some suggestions."

Relief filled her, and Elaine followed Mrs. Harper, noticing the sheriff fell in step behind them. The small crowd that had formed started to break up.

Elaine stopped suddenly and then turned. The two men who'd rushed over to help her still stood nearby, watching. This time, she took a moment to study them. She nodded at Dr. Mason, who watched her with a neutral expression, and then her gaze lingered on his cousin. He was taller than his cousin, younger, and his face was one of worry.

For...for her?

There was a gratitude within her she wasn't sure she'd ever be able to express. How he'd stopped the blow aimed at her, she had no idea.

Elaine stammered as she said, "I didn't thank you, Mr. Mason." Her eyes were locked on his. "I appreciate your help."

"At any time," the doctor assured her, and she glanced at him to give him a small smile.

"Just...just Oliver, please," Mr. Mason said, and she nodded.

Oliver.

Gently, Mrs. Harper guided her away, but Elaine had the strangest feeling wash over her, and she glanced over her shoulder once more. The doctor was walking toward a building, perhaps his office, but Oliver was still looking at her, and Elaine felt...well, she wasn't sure. She didn't understand the expression on his face, but it made a funny little flutter in her stomach.

Elaine pushed that away. She wasn't sure what she should do now, and that must be what took her full focus. Not some stranger who'd protected her. No matter how much she found herself liking him. Wanting to feel the warmth of his touch again.

Chapter 6

Oliver stared through the window of his front room. He'd been working there that morning instead of in his study. He'd told himself it was because he wanted to be able to hear if anyone came to the door, but that wasn't the truth. Not really.

Frequently, his eyes searched the street for the woman who'd been nearly dragged across it yesterday. That evening, Edward had stopped by and told him he'd gone to the boardinghouse to check on her, and she was physically fine, just upset and scared.

Oliver couldn't fault her for that. It also made him realize just how difficult it must be to be a mail-order bride, and be forced to trust a perfect stranger with one's life and wellbeing. Had she ever exchanged letters with the man? Had some idea of who she was coming to meet?

Of course, even if she had, there was the fact that many individuals were dishonest in deed and manner. It could be she'd been lied to. Oliver felt badly for her, and hoped this wouldn't ruin her opinion of the town.

She must have been desperate, there was no other reason for it, because a woman that beautiful, with wavy hair the color of honey and soft green eyes and a desire to seek employment in trade for her room and board could surely have found a husband without going to such extremes.

The thought made something twist in his chest—something uncomfortably like jealousy, which was absurd. He was engaged. He had no right to feel anything at all about Elaine's marital prospects.

He cleared his throat and returned to the notepaper in front of him. Why was it so hard to stay focused today? To keep his thoughts off her? He'd never had this happen before. It must have been because he'd been there, in the middle of the dangerous situation.

"And I was just stating facts," he said in the quiet room, as he thought back to her hair breaking free and falling around her cheeks, the slight parting of her lips. "That's all. I deal in absolutes. It's my job."

But this was the first time he'd ever done such a thing as he had yesterday—stepping between danger and a woman. Truthfully, it was the first time he'd ever come across such a thing, but Oliver was glad he'd reacted, not frozen.

His heart had hammered as he held Harry's fist inches from the woman's face, praying he could stop the man. His arm muscles had trembled, and it had taken all he had in him to stop the man. A flicker had gone through his mind that he might fail, but he knew he couldn't.

She had stared up at him with wide green eyes—terrified, yes, but there was fire in them too. Even shaking, even cornered, she hadn't stopped fighting and he wouldn't either. He found himself not wanting to leave her side, though he knew he should.

Stop. He must stop thinking of her.

With a deep sigh, he hunched over his notepad again and crossed out a line, then rewrote it. With a small frown, he read it once more.

Wanted: A woman to be housekeeper. Meals, cleaning, and answering the door. Room and board included, weekly pay.

That was simple enough. But did he need more? Should he specify that he was a single man right now, but wouldn't be forever? Should he mention the pay? Oliver wasn't quite sure how this worked. He planned to compensate the woman fairly. Whoever she might be. However, he also didn't want to have people arrive just because of a number written on the ad. What if they weren't qualified? It was important to do things properly and interview the woman.

Oliver folded the paper and stood, intending to take it to the small newspaper office. The weekly paper would be printed tomorrow, so perhaps there was a chance to get it in there. He just hoped that whoever answered his job advertisement was someone he could get along with. And honest. You never knew what you would get with a stranger when you were new to town.

Oliver let out a half chuckle as he thought that last part. That was something that he and Elaine had in common.

Elaine. He let himself muse over her name. He couldn't recall if she'd told him her last name, but felt he'd have remembered if she had. He hoped that this morning she was doing well and settled in, as much as she could be.

After taking one more look through the front window, Oliver went to his study to get his money to pay for the ad, and left his home, carefully locking the door behind him.

It was a beautiful late morning. The sun was bright and the sky cloudless. Fresh air filled his lungs and Oliver marveled, as he did each time he walked through Cottonwood Falls, at just how beautiful it was here. He had yet to explore beyond the town, but Edward had promised to show him the winding creek that ran through a wooded area, and some of the best spots for fishing.

"Good morning," a woman passing by greeted Oliver.

"Good morning," he replied, nodding at her.

That was another thing about this town he enjoyed. Everyone nodded or spoke as they passed each other. It was a far cry from the busy town he'd grown up in, where eyes shifted and lips pressed disapprovingly if one didn't appear a certain way.

A shop window caught Oliver's eye, the display of men's shirts sitting in it. "I could use a new shirt or two," he mused. "I should stop by here once I take this advertisement."

As he turned to continue to the newspaper office, he bumped into someone. "Forgive me," Oliver said immediately. "Did I hurt you?"

The woman raised her head, and to his surprise—and delight—it was Elaine. "Not at all," she told him. "It was my fault. I was distracted."

"As was I," he told her, gesturing at the store window. "I admit, I enjoy window shopping and was lost in thought."

She blinked at him in surprise, but then smiled, almost shyly. "That's not something I expected to hear. That a man likes window shopping, I mean."

He laughed. "It's true! I also admire how clever some of the displays are. In Boston, that's where I'm from originally, some of the store windows are like works of art, especially during the holidays. Snowflakes coming from the ceiling, toys and cozy scenes abound, and it's like something out of a storybook."

"Oh! That sounds lovely," Elaine said, her eyes growing a dreamy expression. "I can't even imagine such a thing. It must be wonderful to see."

"It is," Oliver agreed. He hesitated, then ventured, "I'm glad you don't think me foolish."

"Not a bit," she assured him, which made Oliver feel better.

There was silence for a few moments, and then he said, "Are you...settling in? After the terrible events of yesterday?"

"For the most part," Elaine told him. She drew in a shuddering breath. "Though, I will admit that I'm not quite sure just what I should do now."

"Can you return to your family?" Oliver asked. The moment the words escaped, he realized that had been too personal, but as he started to apologize, she answered.

"I have none," Elaine told him. "I have been on my own my whole life."

"I...I'm sorry," he told her. "I shouldn't have pried."

Guilt filled him. Sometimes he spoke without thinking, and this was one of the times that he wished he hadn't. To his surprise, Elaine reached toward him. Her fingers dropped, and she gave a tiny shrug.

Why was it he felt a tug of disappointment when her fingers fell, instead of brushing against him?

"You did not," she told him matter-of-factly. "Had I not wanted to tell you, I wouldn't have."

Her plain way of speaking made Oliver feel relieved. "I appreciate that you don't mince words," he told her. "Too many people pussyfoot about when they are speaking. It makes things confusing to follow along, and to know how they feel."

Elaine gave a soft laugh, and it sounded sweet in his ears. He wondered how he could make her do it again. The sound was almost musical.

He hesitated, then asked, "If I may ask, since you've no family, do you think you will stay here?"

"That depends entirely on if I can find work," Elaine said. "I've quite made up my mind that I've no interest in pursuing the mail-order matrimony thing again. I had my reservations about it already, but I agreed for Lizzie's sake. And, I guess because I had no other options."

"No options?" Oliver repeated, wondering who Lizzie was.

She nodded. "It's quite a long story, but I'd been fine and had a good job at a hotel until about six months ago. When it burned down, I was out of a job and a room. My good friend Lizzie, whom I'd met and roomed with there, was also displaced.

"We found a cheap room and searched for work. However, our savings ran out about four weeks ago. Lizzie was fortunate enough to get a job as a lady's traveling companion, and the same day she learned about the job, she had an offer of marriage from Mr. Smith."

"So you came in her place," Oliver said, piecing everything together. "That way you both had help."

He felt a pang of sympathy for Elaine and her friend. What difficulties they'd had. He wished he had a way to ease them for her.

"That was the plan," Elaine said, "however, as you saw, it has changed suddenly."

Before Oliver could say anything, Elaine continued, "My only choice is to find employment, and think on what I should do in the long term." She glanced around almost wistfully and said, "This seems like a wonderful town, and I think I could be happy here. Well, as long as Mr. Smith doesn't come around."

"If he does," Oliver said as a wave of protectiveness washed over him, "please tell me. Or my cousin, Dr. Mason. We won't let him bother you."

"Mrs. Harper said the same," Elaine said, "and I am grateful for it." Her feet shuffled, and she said, "I must be going now. I'm going business to business to see who might hire me."

She walked off, and Oliver waved goodbye. He hoped she could find something. Cottonwood Falls was of a good size, for a small town, but it didn't have the most jobs to offer. Or the most seeking them, which was why he hoped he'd be able to find himself a housekee—

"Elaine!" Oliver called suddenly.

When she paused and looked over her shoulder, Oliver jogged over to her. "I apologize. I don't know your last name."

"It's Winters," she told him, "but Elaine is quite fine."

"Elaine," he agreed, liking the way her name sounded on his lips. "I was on my way to the newspaper office to place an ad," he told her, pulling it out so that she would see he was telling the truth. "I'm looking for a housekeeper. If you want it, the job is yours."

Elaine looked over the paper, and then studied him. Her eyes searched his face for a moment, and Oliver wondered what she was looking for. His heart was racing strangely. Was he unwell? He'd need to ask Edward.

Finally, she asked, "A housekeeper for just you?"

"Yes. Well, for right now," he stammered. "I-I have an intended, and she will be here within a few weeks. Once we marry, it will be for the both of us. I'd pay you twelve dollars a week. Plus, your meals and room."

She blinked several times, and then nodded. "May I think on it?" Elaine asked him.

"Of course! You are new here, and don't know me. Take whatever time you need. If we don't cross paths again, my office, and my home, is right there."

He pointed to the small building with the wooden frame he'd recently whitewashed, and the sleek black painted door with his sign right nearby.

"Thank you," Elaine said. She offered the paper he'd written the ad on, but he shook his head. "You can keep it. If you decide you don't want the job, then I'll take it back so it can go into the newspaper."

Elaine nodded. "Thank you."

She walked away then, glancing over her shoulder once and giving him a small smile before she headed toward the general store.

Oliver tried not to sigh. Of course she was headed there. She likely wasn't interested in his job, and he sure couldn't blame her. She was probably scared, what with her being new to town and him being single. That's why he'd mentioned Melanie. Hoping it would put her at ease.

Of course, there might be an issue when Melanie arrived if Elaine did take the job, with how lovely she was. With how easy she was to talk to. With how her laugh made something warm unfurl in his chest.

Not that Oliver had noticed any of those things, of course.

Chapter 7

Elaine was aware that Oliver watched her as she walked away. It didn't bother her, though. He might be a near stranger, but she felt that she could trust him. That he wasn't going to harm her. Which was why his offer of letting her be his housekeeper was so appealing. So was the twelve dollars a week plus room and meals.

Then, her eyes narrowed. Why was he willing to pay that much? It seemed a little too generous. Did he expect something more in trade? Why, back at the hotel, her wage was six dollars a week, plus room and meals. This was double. And, she'd be the one in charge of running the place. Was that why? There would be much more responsibility?

Elaine paused in front of the general store, but didn't go inside. Instead, she snuck a look over her shoulder to see Oliver walking away. Feeling safe enough to study him without his notice, she did.

His offer was very appealing, but she wasn't sure what to do. Slowly, Elaine turned and headed back to the boardinghouse. She wanted time to think and ask questions, and the boardinghouse owner would be good for that second part.

Mrs. Harper seemed a lovely woman, and though they'd just met, it was obvious she knew everything about everyone in the town. It would be very helpful to get her input and advice on the situation, and if she felt Oliver could be trusted.

It wasn't a far walk to the boardinghouse, a multi-story yellow building with a white door, flowers in pots on the front porch, and some rocking chairs that were a little worn sitting near them.

A sign hung by the door read: *Rooms for rent.* When she'd asked, she was told there were currently four other boarders, one being the sheriff she'd met yesterday. Truthfully, the idea made her feel much better about staying here.

She'd been grateful the other woman had taken her in yesterday. Though she had trouble falling asleep, it wasn't due to the comfortable bed or the wonderful meal of carrot and corn stew she'd been full with.

The sheriff had told Elaine it was unlikely Mr. Smith would be bothering her, especially with him locked in the jail right now. When she had admitted her worry that he might end up coming after her once he was released, the sheriff had told her Mr. Smith had a stack of mail-order bride letters in his pocket, and women had been arriving most every day. She was the only one he'd gotten aggressive with. The sheriff figured it was only a matter of time before he ended up with one who tolerated him.

Elaine had thought that was horrible, and Mrs. Harper had agreed, but then she said there was someone for everyone, and she suspected there was a woman who'd be thrilled with a farmer such as he was. While Elaine herself wasn't too sure about that, she did feel safe enough, knowing that several people had promised to help if she needed it, and also were keeping an eye on her.

However, Elaine also knew she couldn't entirely depend on them or anyone else, and that she'd have to take care of herself. If only she knew what to do. The entire situation was stressful, and for a moment, she wished she'd never come here.

As she pushed open the boardinghouse door and let herself inside, Elaine followed her nose to the kitchen, where the spicy scent of ginger and cinnamon met her.

"Hello, dear," Mrs. Harper said. "I'm just making some cookies."

"May I help?" Elaine asked. "Remember, I've got to earn my way."

"Don't worry about that just now," the older woman told her. "When I set to tidying the main rooms today, I'll get your help. Also with dinner. For now, why don't you have some tea, a few of the cookies, and tell me what's on your mind? It's written all over your face."

"Is it?" Elaine asked, peering at her reflection in the kitchen window and trying to see what the other woman saw.

"Yes. So, don't keep me in suspense!" Mrs. Harper brought over some tea and a plate of cookies. "Tell me what's got that pretty face of yours all worried looking."

Elaine wasn't sure how to start, so she just blurted out the first thing that came to mind. "I was offered a job."

"Already? Wonderful!" Mrs. Harper said. "What sort?"

"That's the part that has me worried," Elaine admitted. "Do you remember those two men yesterday? The doctor and his cousin?"

"I do."

"Well, Mr. Oliver Mason offered me a job as his housekeeper." Elaine paused, and wrapped her hands around the mug before her. "Can I get your opinion of him?"

"I am full of opinions!" the boardinghouse owner said, her tone delighted. She leaned back slightly. "Let's see...Oliver Mason. He's a fine young man, moved here recently to Cottonwood Falls to open his accounting business. I can tell you more about his cousin, the doctor, who is a cornerstone of our community, but Oliver also seems like a fine man. What has you worried?"

"I guess just because he's offered me room and board and twelve dollars a week. Cooking, cleaning, and answering the door." Elaine hesitated. "It seems...too good to be true."

"Hm. I'm sure he has it," Mrs. Harper said. "And I recall hearing that the woman he is to marry is coming soon. And that she's rather fussy. You didn't hear that from me, though. Likely she is demanding a housekeeper, and you might be earning every bit of that twelve dollars. That all said, at least ten a week should be the rate for a small place such as his. Until she arrives, you can continue to lodge here. I assume you weren't going to stay there without another woman in the house?"

"I was not," Elaine said. "I worry about talk, you know? Neither of us being married."

"It would be more convenient for you staying there," Mrs. Harper said, "and him being a man, he might not have thought this fully through, but I agree, it's best you not be there overnight, without another woman. You being so young and all. People do talk. I'm sure he'd be happy regardless if you continue to board here. It's the help he needs. He'd be able to make do for a few hours overnight."

Elaine nodded. "It bears consideration. I'm not sure yet. I'd want to see my room and make sure it has a lock for when she does arrive and I stay there. But you feel he is upstanding?"

"I do," the housekeeper said, then sniffed the air and rose. "Last batch of cookies is done. Will you give me a hand in the sitting room? I want to dust and beat the rugs. We can continue talking while we work."

"I will start right away," Elaine said, finishing the last of her tea and biting into one more cookie.

She left with the dusting rag in hand, and started to wipe down the sitting room. Though her arrival had started a bit roughly, things seemed to be more promising today. She'd have to write Lizzie, and let her know that she wasn't marrying, but instead was taking a job. She'd be sure to leave out the frightening parts. She didn't want to make her friend feel bad, but Elaine was quite glad that she had an option now. A few days ago, she had none. Well, none besides marrying a stranger.

"If you'll help me take these rugs out and beat the dust from them, it won't take us much longer," Mrs. Harper said.

"What would you like me to help with next?" Elaine asked, once she'd gotten the rugs hung out on the line. She picked up the carpet beater and struck the carpet steadily, watching as specks of dust and dirt flew away and into the air. When the wind switched directions, so did she.

"I don't need anything else until dinnertime," Mrs. Harper said. "After all, you helped me change the linens already and get them bagged up for the woman who does the washing."

"Then perhaps I will go seek out Mr. Mason, tell him I accept the position," Elaine said. "Conditionally, as I would prefer to stay here, at least until there is another woman in the home."

"I am sure he will understand the reasonableness in that," Mrs. Harper said. "Just help me get these back inside with that young, strong body of yours, and you can be off."

Elaine carried the rugs back inside, spread them out, and then went to wash off her face and hands. She glanced down at her dress, but decided against changing out of it. This was her nicest dress, and she'd worn it in hopes of getting a job. Her others were plain, getting worn, and she longed for a few new ones.

If Oliver did decide to hire her, with this job, she'd not only be able to get the fabric to make a dress, but she'd also perhaps make two!

It didn't take her long to walk to the house Oliver had pointed out. She hesitated, and then knocked. The door opened almost immediately, and he stood before her, hair slightly messy, a smear of ink on his cheek. It took a surprising amount of strength not to reach up and wipe at it.

"Hello," Oliver said, almost breathlessly.

Elaine felt just the same, and didn't quite know what that meant. "Hello," she answered, hoping her voice would come out steadily. "I came about the job. If you are still offering it."

"I—you—yes! I am!" His eyes were wide, his voice stammering, as though he couldn't believe she was here. It was endearing, and she couldn't stop the small smile that formed. "Come inside. Please."

He stood to the side as she walked in. "Welcome to my home," he said. "Let me show you around?"

Elaine nodded, and accepted the quick tour. She followed him from room to room, and it wasn't a large place so she couldn't imagine it would be too difficult a job. She asked each question as it came to her mind, and as he showed her the room that would be hers, voiced her concern about staying there.

Quickly, he agreed to her decision that she'd prefer to stay at the boardinghouse until his intended arrived, though she'd take some meals with him here. Once they'd sorted out all of the details, Elaine agreed to start in the morning.

He walked her to the door, and as he opened it and Elaine stepped into the sunshine, she froze. There, walking nearby, was Mr. Smith. He didn't seem to notice her, but Elaine trembled in fear. Why was he just walking around?

Oliver stepped closer to her. He rested his hand on the small of her back. The warmth of his palm seeped through the fabric of her dress, and Elaine's breath caught. She shouldn't lean into his touch, shouldn't find such comfort in it, but she did. For a moment, she let herself imagine what it would be like if he were something more than her employer.

His voice was low, protective, as he said, "I won't let anyone hurt you. If need be, I will walk you both ways each day."

She longed to accept, but that wouldn't have been practical for him. It also might lead to gossip, and he was a man with his future wife arriving soon. She couldn't do that to him or to the woman. So, she just shook her head, and said, "I'll be fine, but I appreciate your offer."

Oliver's warm eyes looked into hers, and time seemed to slow. Elaine was sure her eyes had widened, and she felt as though it was hard to catch her breath. Something flickered in his gaze—something intense and unguarded—before he blinked and looked away, his jaw clenching.

They stood like that for a moment before she reluctantly whispered goodbye and left, hurrying over to the boardinghouse. Perhaps working for Oliver wasn't a good idea. Not when he set her heart thumping the way it was doing right now.

What was wrong with her? He was to be married. But the unexpected small voice that kept whispering she wished it was to her, filled her ears, making her heart beat even faster.

Chapter 8

Only a few days had passed since Elaine had come to work for him. She arrived early each morning and made breakfast for him, then tidied up his house or made some sort of treat in the kitchen. She'd told Oliver her skills were limited, but she was eager to expand on them, and Oliver didn't mind her experimentations at all.

The odd time someone came to the door, she answered it politely and professionally, and showed the person to his study, bringing in refreshments if he asked for them.

Oliver had gained a new client just yesterday, and hoped to get another before much longer. Until then, he threw himself into his work, doing the best job that he could for the clients he had, even if he had far more hours on his hands than he'd have liked.

It was quite nice though, not to feel that restless silence of his house. Now, there was the faint sound of Elaine moving about, or a wonderful smell coming from the kitchen. She'd offered to bring his meals to the study, and that's often where he had breakfast and lunch, but today for his lunch, he wanted to have it with her.

Oliver told himself it was because he wanted to check in, to see how she was finding the job, but really, he wanted to enjoy her company. The realization made something twist uncomfortably in his chest. He was engaged. He shouldn't be seeking out Elaine's company like this.

"It's just a meal. Some conversation," he said out loud, trying to justify the plan. "After all, Elaine might be lonely. She doesn't know anyone here. This would be a good chance to ask her how things are going, and if she is enjoying her job."

That *was* the truth. And if he enjoyed sharing a meal with her...he couldn't help it. He was a little lonely too. Guilt rose, but he pushed it aside and headed to the kitchen.

As he walked the short distance from his study, he tried to puzzle out the meal from the wonderful smells filling his nose. Just as he walked into the kitchen, his stomach let out a loud rumble.

Elaine turned from the stove, amusement on her face as she laughed, "Someone's hungry!"

His cheeks warmed, and he apologized, "I am. Goodness, but that was embarrassing!"

"It was flattering," she corrected him. "I'm not the world's best cook, but I can manage, and Mrs. Harper has been wonderful to share some of her recipes and advice with me. That's helped tremendously."

"I thought I'd eat in here today, if that's all right with you?" Oliver asked. "Perhaps have lunch with you?"

Her back was to him so he couldn't see what her expression was, but Elaine answered, "Sure. It's almost done. It's shepherd's pie and apple cake."

"I'll just wait here then," he told her, sitting at the small kitchen table. There was a small dining room, but he preferred his meals here.

It wasn't long at all before she had the food before him, and sat across from him. Oliver ate several bites before he asked, "How are you finding things here?"

"Well enough," Elaine answered. "In truth, you don't give me much to do!"

"Are you terribly bored?" he asked.

She scooped up a bite into her fork. "Not really. Sometimes it feels strange not to have nonstop tasks, but it leaves me more time to practice my cooking skills and improve upon them. I did want to ask, I saw you had quite a few books. Would you mind if I borrowed one to read while I was cooking? I'd be very careful, but I thought I could prop it while I'm kneading bread or stirring things."

"Take any you like," Oliver told her earnestly. Then he added, "But if you have free time, which I know you do right now, please, relax and enjoy the book. I won't mind."

Her brows knitted together and Elaine said, "You aren't paying me to sit around."

He chuckled. "I'm not the kind of man to make you work every second! As long as the meals are done, the door answered, and the house tidy, that's all I want."

"Most wouldn't say that," Elaine answered in surprise.

Unbidden, Melanie's face came to mind—her perfectly arranged curls, her critical gaze, the way she'd looked at him with disappointment when he'd told her about moving here. He pushed the image away, uncomfortable with how easily Elaine's warm presence made him forget about his fiancée entirely. However, she was right. Melanie might not be fond of seeing Elaine rest. He needed to remedy that.

"When Melanie arrives, please don't feel you have to wait on her. She has a maid she is bringing with her. I've already written and told her that I have you, but that your job is to care for the house's needs. Just so there's no question about it."

Elaine nodded. "Will you tell me some about her? So I know what to expect?"

Oliver hesitantly told Elaine about the woman he was to marry. What she looked like, how she liked to travel, and ride horses, and see theatre productions. Her fondness for music and poetry, and long walks.

He wasn't sure why he was reluctant to share anything beyond the surface level of their relationship. Was it because he was worried about what Elaine would think?

The realization hit him like a stone—he wanted Elaine to think well of him. Wanted her to see him as... as what? A good man? An honorable one? Not someone trapped in an engagement he'd been talked into?

The thought was dangerous, and he forced himself to keep talking about Melanie, though every word felt like a betrayal. Of whom, he wasn't sure.

"We have horses, at least," Elaine said thoughtfully once he'd stopped. "It will be quite a journey to see the theatre. Though if she likes to travel, perhaps that will not be a problem. There are walks aplenty to be had, and poetry books, though I don't care much for them myself."

"I just hope she will find happiness here," he said quietly. "I worry she may not. This is a lovely place, but nothing like she's accustomed to."

"You are a good person to be so concerned, Oliver," Elaine said.

Her eyes searched his face, and Oliver felt as though she were looking deeply into his soul. Seeing him. It was a strange feeling, but he also didn't mind. With Elaine, he wasn't uncomfortable. From the moment she'd started working there, it had felt relaxed. Easy. Something he hoped would last.

"I imagine she..." Oliver stopped. What had he been about to say? That he imagined Melanie would find something to occupy her time? He wondered what her maid was like. She was on her second this year.

"It's all right," Elaine said softly, her hand lying overtop his for a moment.

Oliver froze. Her fingers were warm, gentle, and for a fraction of a second, he didn't dare move, afraid she'd pull away. When she finally did, lifting her hand to the locket at her throat, he felt the loss of her touch like a physical ache. His palm still tingled where she'd touched him.

Elaine continued, her voice slightly strained. "You don't have to explain. I am an adult and well aware that in life, we don't always get to choose how things work out, and sometimes we have to settle or make do. I sense that might be the situation here. However, whatever I can do to ease things for you, I will."

His eyes tore from the hand she'd removed, and the words seemed caught in his throat as he tried to mumble a thank you. Was it so obvious to her as well as to Edward that he had such apprehension about his future with Melanie? With her desire and capability to live here?

"Congratulations on your newest client," Elaine said, changing the subject.

"Thank you," he told her, as he latched onto the subject. "I hope to have ten by the end of the month. It turns out there's a man not too far away by the name of Andrew Radcliffe, and he and his wife Evie are looking to hire someone. It's possible that he might recommend me to others if I do well enough. There's a man who raises horses around these parts too, named Aaron Woods. I understand he and his wife Rosalee might also welcome help."

"Rosalee was one of Mrs. Harper's boarders," Elaine said, her face lighting up. "Why, her husband too. Mrs. Harper was telling me their story the other day. It was terribly romantic."

"I'll have to hear it from you later," Oliver told her.

She nodded, then said, "I'm sure that before too long, why, you'll have so many clients you might have to turn some away."

"From your lips to God's ears," Oliver groaned. "I really don't want to go back to Boston."

"Is that something that might happen?" Elaine asked, and he didn't miss her worried expression. Was it because she feared for her job? Or...might miss him? He hoped for the second, but didn't know why he'd even wondered such a thing. Melanie. He had Melanie.

"I must make money in order to keep my business going," he said. "I fear it might be harder in a small town, but Edward and Caroline think I'll be all right once I get established."

"Who is Caroline?" Elaine asked.

"That's my cousin's wife. She's a doctor too."

"How wonderful!" Elaine gasped.

"I think so," Oliver agreed. "You'd have never known that she grew up in an orphanage without the support she needed early in her life."

To his surprise, Elaine's eyes filled with tears. Before he could ask what was wrong, she whispered, her eyes downward, "I did too. I struggle terribly sometimes thinking that I'm all alone, when everyone else seems to have someone they are connected to. The worst part is that when people find out you were in an orphanage, they either think you are useless, because your parents abandoned you, or else that you are no good and will cause problems."

"I'm so sorry," Oliver said, horrified at the turn the conversation had taken. That was probably another of the reasons that she'd come here to marry a stranger. Elaine was without family. "I'd never think such a thing about you!" he hastened to assure her.

She gave him a watery smile, and took a deep breath, then a bite of her lunch, visibly steeling herself. It made him wonder how many times over the years she'd had to do that. Comfort herself.

"Thank you. But don't be sorry," Elaine said a moment later, squeezing her fist again around the locket. "From the start, I felt like I could trust you not to think poorly about me. And after hearing that story, somehow, I feel better. If Caroline became a doctor after such a difficult beginning in life, who knows what will happen to me? I will find my way as well."

"You will," Oliver agreed. "However I can help you, I will."

"Thank you," Elaine said softly.

They ate in silence for a time, and then he remarked, "The necklace you wear. I feel like I've seen it before."

"Have you?" Elaine looked down. "It's only half a locket. It's broken in two. But it was my mother's, I was told."

"Maybe she still has the other part," Oliver said.

"Maybe. I try not to think about her, it's too painful, but I do wonder why she left me. I hope...I hope it wasn't because she didn't want me."

Oliver's chest felt tight, like he was sure Elaine's must be. He reached for her hand this time, covering it with his own.

Her fingers were small and work-worn beneath his palm, and when she didn't pull away, something in his chest expanded. They sat like that for a long moment, her hand in his, neither of them speaking. He knew he should let go. Knew this was crossing a line he had no right to cross. But he couldn't seem to make himself release her.

"Don't assume the worst, that you were abandoned." Oliver looked into her eyes. "Sometimes, we must do things we don't always want to. It's like you said, we don't always get to choose how things work out. It is possible that was your mother's situation, and she did whatever she could to see you to a safe place, where you'd grow to adulthood, with food and clothing and an education."

"I think you are right," Elaine said, looking sadly into her empty bowl. "I hope you are, anyway."

"I feel sure of it. You are a wonderful woman, Elaine, and I think you have no idea just how incredible you are."

Her eyes met his, and the room felt charged. Heavy with something that Oliver felt filling every inch of him. It was potent, scary, and he replayed the words he'd just said in his mind. It had been a confession of sorts. This was dangerous. He should pull his hand away. Stand up. Make an excuse to return to his study. But Elaine was looking at him with those soft green eyes, and he found he couldn't move. Couldn't break whatever spell had fallen over them.

It was Elaine who finally pulled her hand free, her cheeks flushed as she stood and began clearing the dishes. Oliver forced himself to thank her for the meal and retreat to his study, but his hand still burned where she'd touched him.

What was happening? Worse, what had he done? He'd fallen in love.

Chapter 9

Elaine peered into the oven at the sweet loaf that was baking, then used the edge of her apron to pull it from the rack. The scent of nutmeg, cinnamon, and plump raisins smacked her face and she breathed in deeply.

Hunger had been the furthest thing from her mind since she'd arrived. Oliver encouraged her to enjoy as much food or drink as she'd like, and told her that when she did the weekly shopping it was important for her to get the things she liked too.

His kindness and generosity were almost overwhelming, but Elaine tried not to read too much into it. He was simply being a good employer, that was all. It was nothing more, no matter how she'd wish for things to be otherwise.

Elaine was ashamed of her thoughts. Not for the first—or fiftieth—time she reminded herself he belonged to someone else, even if there seemed to be some reluctance on that front. She wasn't the sort of woman to do such a thing as go after someone else's man. Besides, he wouldn't ever be interested in someone such as her—an orphan with no family, no connections, no dowry. Melanie probably had all those things. Of course he'd chosen someone like her.

Then, there was also the fact they'd only known each other a short time. He might have flattered her when he'd called her wonderful and told her how incredible she was, but that was just Oliver being kind. Trying to make her feel better. He had, but oh, how she wished the circumstances had been slightly different.

Elaine had never experienced heartache in a romantic sense, but she'd also never met anyone like him. Kind, thoughtful, intellectual, and the kind of person she just couldn't stop thinking about.

Oliver rushed in, a dab of ink on his face and his hair wild. "Elaine!" He dropped a ledger on the table, open. "I'm expecting a potential client. Edward just stuck his head in the window to tell me. Would you be able to bring us—" He stopped and his eyes fell on the loaf. "What is that wonderful looking thing?"

"Cinnamon raisin bread," Elaine said. "Another recipe from Mrs. Harper. Shall I bring some of it and some coffee to your study once your potential client arrives?"

"Please," he told her. "I'll be in my study."

"Wait!" Elaine called out, putting her hand on his arm to halt him. He looked at her confused, and it was all she could do not to reach up and wipe the smudge off his face or smooth his hair. For such a serious man, he also had his moments of absolute charm in his absentmindedness.

She gestured to him. "Perhaps you should get the ink off your face and comb your hair first."

He strode out of the kitchen and she could see him peer into the small hallway mirror, and his eyes grow wide. "Thank you, Elaine!" he called out as he dashed up the stairs to his room. "Once again, you've saved me!"

The laughter she'd held in escaped. Over the last few days, he'd used that phrase quite a bit. It seemed that Oliver was many things, including brilliant with numbers, but he was a little forgetful about his own needs. She was more than happy to see he was fed and looked after. Would his fiancée do the same? She hoped so.

Elaine removed the loaf from the pan, willing it to cool quickly so that she could slice it more easily. Her gaze fell on the ledger, and she picked it up, walking into the hallway to return it to him.

Just then, Oliver appeared, still looking a little flushed from his haste, but ink and rumpled-hair free. There was a knock at the door, and Elaine said, "I'll let them in, and bring your coffee and bread."

"Thank you," Oliver said. He took the book, and the brush of his fingers against hers set her to tingling terribly.

Drawing a deep breath and trying to hide her sudden shakiness, Elaine walked to the door and let in the older man who was clutching a stack of loose papers.

"Good morning," she greeted him. "If you'll follow me? Mr. Mason is expecting you."

Once she'd led the man to the study, she told Oliver, "I'll bring your coffee in, and then do a few errands."

He nodded his thanks, and stooped to help the man with his papers that were floating to the floor. In the kitchen, Elaine loaded a tray with cups, the coffee pot, and slices of the cinnamon raisin bread on plates, then took it to the study, placing it on Oliver's desk before slipping out.

She glanced at the list of jobs she needed to do, and decided to leave for the seamstress in town. Oliver had requested some new shirts and had given her his measurements. Elaine was grateful for the distraction of tasks, even if some did pertain to him. Dwelling on Oliver and his impending marriage would only make the ache in her chest worse. Better to keep busy. Better to focus on practical matters like shirts and fabric or meals and sundries.

It wasn't difficult to locate the small shop of the seamstress. In the front window she had two men's shirts, a woman's dress, and a shawl. Elaine decided to see how much she might charge to make some dresses. Until now, she'd made most of her own, but she would like to have something a little nicer than the simple designs she could create, if it was somewhat affordable.

Elaine pushed open the door and walked in, her eyes going right to the various fabrics in stacks along the wall.

"Be right with you," a woman's voice called from the back.

"Take your time," Elaine answered, and wandered toward a beautiful lavender-striped print.

There was the sound of footsteps, and she turned to see a woman in an apron, with scissors in her pocket and a measuring tape around her neck. Though she wore a smile as she greeted Elaine, there was a lingering sadness on her face that seemed to speak of years of sorrow. Elaine recognized it at once. The same expression often stared back at her in the mirror.

"My employer would like some new shirts," Elaine said, offering the slip of paper with Oliver's measurements. "And, I wondered how much a dress for me might run."

"It depends on the fabric and the style," the seamstress answered.

"This fabric?" Elaine asked, reaching for the one that had caught her eye. "In the style in the window?" She held her breath, sure it would be far more than she could afford.

"Twelve dollars," the seamstress answered.

Elaine nearly gasped. She could afford it! How wonderful it would be to have a custom-made dress. "I'd love to be measured if you have time."

"Of course," the woman said. "I'm Sally Manders. Let me write down your employer's order, then I will help you."

"Thank you. I think I'd like a few dresses," Elaine said. "Some everyday work suited ones? If it's no trouble? I've never had one made for me before. But with my new job, and the fact that my dresses are starting to become threadbare, I'd love to get a few before I look indecent. I think having you make them, they'd look better than ones I could make. I try, but I'm not a very good seamstress."

"It's no trouble at all," Sally told her. She went to the wall of fabrics and pulled down several. A soft green, a light blue, and one that was cream with small golden flowers on it. "These fabrics are good for daily wear. I've others too, but I thought these might suit your complexion. In a dress style similar to what you are wearing, they would be six dollars each."

"That's all?" Elaine asked, her brow furrowing. "Surely, it must take you a good deal of time to sew."

The woman smiled. "I have a machine! It speeds things up tremendously."

"It sounds so extravagant," Elaine said, "but could I have the purple stripe, the same as in the window, and then day dresses, in these three fabrics? You chose well. I like each of them."

"Let me take your measurements," the woman said, leading Elaine to the back room.

Elaine held still while Sally measured here and there, jotting down the lengths.

"You've not had a new dress for a while?" the seamstress asked.

"No. The last dress I had that was new was about four years ago. I made myself two with money I'd made at my last job, right after I left the orphanage. Before that, I wore hand-me-downs."

The woman's hands stilled. "O-orphanage, you say?"

"Yes," Elaine said softly. "I'd been there since I was a baby."

The other woman swallowed visibly hard, then said, "I'm sorry. It must have been difficult to be on your own. To grow up without family."

"At times," Elaine said. "But I was fortunate that there were good people there caring for us. We might not have had much, but we had a roof and meals, and an education."

"Which orphanage were you in, if you don't mind my asking?" Sally said.

"Sunshine Acres," Elaine said.

The pencil dropped from Sally's fingers, and she scrambled after it. The woman seemed quite nervous, and Elaine wondered why. Perhaps she'd never met an orphan, and thought they were dangerous. She hoped that wasn't it. Should she reassure her that she harbored no ill intentions?

"There," Sally said, writing the last measurement down and pulling Elaine from that thought. She smiled, though it didn't quite meet her eyes, and she said, "I will work on all of these and get them to you as quickly as possible."

Feeling a little awkward now, Elaine thanked her and left. As she stepped back outside, and glanced to be sure the door had closed behind her, she could feel the seamstress watching her. She tried not to let it disturb her. After all, she'd done nothing wrong. But why else had the woman acted so startled?

As she walked back to Oliver's home, Elaine felt grateful that he'd taken a chance on her. Perhaps not everyone in Cottonwood Falls would be as welcoming, now that they would know she was an orphan and potentially of bad stock. She'd never felt less before, not knowing her parentage, but now she did.

Chapter 10

It was hard not to whistle as he walked to the post office, but Oliver couldn't help it. He was in such a good mood! Mr. Roth had come into his study with an armful of papers, a dour expression, and a whole lot of doubt about Oliver's capability to bring order to that chaos—and had left a client.

Things were looking up, and he was feeling much more optimistic about his future here. He was settling in, and Elaine... he was so glad he'd hired her. She was an enormous help, plus someone he enjoyed talking to. The only thing that kept flitting through his mind were the what-if questions.

What if Melanie didn't like her? What if Melanie treated her poorly, and Elaine left?

Oliver felt oddly protective of Elaine. He wasn't sure why that was, but he'd felt that way since the moment he'd first laid eyes on her. It had only grown, and to the point that now, after two weeks of having her in his home during the daylight hours, he couldn't imagine life without her.

It wasn't just because of her upbringing and how alone she must have felt. He wasn't even sure if it was because she hadn't let that slow her, and had done the best she could to make a life for herself. Frankly, Oliver wasn't sure what it was, but he didn't want Elaine to leave.

"Letters for you, Mr. Mason," the postmaster said, reaching into a mail slot and handing him three envelopes.

Oliver took them and flipped through the mail quickly. One was from an old friend, another from his mother. The last was from Melanie. He didn't know why, there was no reason at all for it, but Oliver's mood drooped when he saw it.

Drooped might have been too polite a word. It more than sank. It crashed.

A strange anxiety filled him, the likes of which had been happening each time he had a letter from Melanie, and he opened the envelope and read the short note.

I arrive on Wednesday. My maid will be accompanying me, and I look forward to meeting the housekeeper you have hired for us. This is a list of the items I'd like ready for my arrival. Mother and Father have been delayed, and we will wait to be wed once they arrive.

He couldn't help but feel the slightest bit of relief at the delay in the marriage. Though, now there was concern over the list Melanie wanted. Oliver ran his eyes down the sheet of paper, then over to the backside, and then the additional page that was attached. Was there anything Melanie hadn't asked for? He wasn't even sure if the general store sold all of this. Perhaps Elaine would know.

He jammed the letter—if one could call so few lines that—and the list into the envelope and headed home. As he walked inside, he could hear Elaine bustling about in the sitting room. Oliver poked his head in and found her standing on a chair, a cleaning cloth in one hand, and her balance quite precarious.

"Be careful!" he said.

However, his warning didn't have the intended effect. Elaine startled at his voice and slipped from the chair.

There was a terrifying moment when everything seemed to both stand still and move too quickly. Oliver flung himself toward her, and somehow managed to catch her before she tumbled to the floor. For a breathless moment, she was in his arms, her weight against his chest, her face mere inches from his own. Her eyes—those soft green eyes—were wide with surprise, and he could feel the rapid rise and fall of her breathing. Or was that his own heart hammering?

"I'm so sorry," he managed, lowering her gently to her feet but unable to make himself let go entirely. His hands still held her arms, steadying her. "Are you hurt?"

She shook her head, though she didn't quite meet his eyes, and he realized with a start that she was trembling. "Not at all," she whispered.

He should let go. He knew he should. But for one long moment, neither of them moved. Then Elaine's gaze dropped to where his hands still held her, and he hastily released her, stepping back as though burned.

Stammering, he said, "I just wanted to let you know, I had a letter from Melanie. She'll be here Wednesday. Her parents hope to be here a few days after."

"That's wonderful," Elaine said, finally meeting his eyes.

Her smile didn't quite seem as bright as it usually was. He must have upset her, embarrassed her, maybe even alarmed her with his impropriety in holding her hands so intimately. Oliver felt terrible. What must she think of him?

He offered Melanie's letter, hoping to dispel some of the awkward tension in the room, and said, "She has a large list of items she wants. But I don't know if the store has them all. Or if we have some of it already. Would you take a look?"

"Of course," Elaine said, seemingly glad for something to do. She took the list, scanned it, and he didn't miss her expression as it flickered between a combination of disbelief, amusement, and exasperation. "This is the longest list I've ever seen."

Oliver grimaced. "The future might hold worse. Just get it. Whatever is on there. If you can. I will figure out something for the rest. There are other towns. Perhaps I can special order."

Elaine nodded, and returned the list to the envelope. "I'll start now. It may need to be delivered; I don't think I can carry it all."

"Of course. Whatever you need to do to make things easier for yourself. Thank you," Oliver said.

She slipped past him so quietly, he could hear the whisper of her skirt. The faint scent of lilac brushed against his nose. A few seconds later, the front door closed, and Oliver realized he'd been standing there frozen, thinking of her in his arms.

His eyes sought her through the window, and he watched as Elaine crossed the street. He wanted to make sure she got there safely. That was all. Wasn't it?

There was no more danger from the man she'd arrived to marry. Mr. Smith had actually left town. Sold his farm and became a mail-order husband, to everyone's surprise. The sheriff had told them so a few days ago, so Elaine should have been free to walk without worry.

But it was he who had that emotion now.

He had to stop. Stop this feeling that was growing. The one that made him want to tell Melanie he was sorry. That it wouldn't work out. He longed to tell her that anyway. Oliver knew the two of them weren't right for each other. But it didn't matter. He'd offered his hand in marriage, pledged himself to her, and he was a man of his word.

Besides, it was quite obvious, by Elaine's uncomfortable mannerism, that she wouldn't have been interested in him. Which was better, Oliver wondered? To be alone, when the one you loved didn't care for you? Or to be wed to someone who wouldn't love you?

He knew the answer. He'd always known. But knowing didn't change the fact that Melanie would arrive soon, and he would marry her, do his best to be a kind and loving husband, but also be forced to spend the rest of his life pretending he didn't love Elaine Winters.

Chapter 11

Elaine's heart was still pounding as she studied Melanie's list. She told herself it was from nearly falling, from the scare of losing her balance. But that wasn't the truth.

It was from being in Oliver's arms.

For a moment she wished she could have frozen time. She'd been pressed against his chest, his face so close she could have counted his eyelashes.

And when he'd steadied her, his hands warm and strong on her arms, she'd been unable to move, unable to breathe, unable to think of anything except how badly she'd wanted him to pull her closer instead of letting go. Elaine had never felt such a thing before. Of all the terrible times for this to happen. And with someone who was promised to another.

Heat flooded her cheeks even now, standing alone in the general store. What was wrong with her? Oliver was engaged. Engaged. And she was mooning over him like some foolish girl. She needed to stop. Needed to focus on the task at hand. Melanie's list. Elaine prayed it would clear her head.

The list that Oliver gave her wasn't just several pages. It was several pages of specific items and brands in the smallest, neatest handwriting Elaine had ever seen. It made her even more curious about the woman he was to marry. If she was this exacting in her list, what was she like in person?

"Goodness," the woman at the general store said, squinting at the list. "I think we have some of this. Let me start to gather it, and then I'll mark the items I need to order."

"Thank you," Elaine said. "If it's a manageable amount that you have in the store, I'll carry it back. Otherwise, I'm afraid I'll need it delivered."

"Of course," the woman said, walking around the store, paper in hand. "I might be a little while. Did you wish to browse? Or come back?"

"I'll browse around," Elaine answered.

She meandered through the store, soaking in all of the wonderful items there. Oliver had often told her to choose whatever she needed to run the household, including more cooking items, and so that's what she planned to do today. While ordinarily she'd have tried to make do, with additional people arriving soon, and the potential for them to have others over for dinner, his single frying pan and small pot just wouldn't be enough.

Elaine had never spent so much at once. It didn't matter it wasn't her money, she was still conscious of the prices as she selected three new pieces of cookware—another larger frying pan and pot, and then a large Dutch oven—and studied the baking tins.

Thanks to Mrs. Harper, she was feeling both more confident and comfortable in the kitchen. She also found she enjoyed Oliver's reactions when she made him meals. He appreciated simple food, and had told her he liked being able to relax without worrying over which fork was used for what.

She'd had to have him explain what he meant, and had laughed when he told her that he'd been to several meals where they were seated at a table with more forks and spoons than he had fingers. What a silly thing that was! Couldn't a body use the same fork and spoon throughout the entirety of the meal? Even if there were several dishes served?

When she'd asked that, he hadn't made her feel foolish, but instead had agreed, and told her that he wished that was the case. He'd have saved himself the horrified looks from others when he used the wrong fork for the wrong food. That was another thing she'd laughed at.

How very different Boston must be! She didn't imagine she'd ever go there, but if she did, she hoped she'd be able to avoid putting herself in such situations. She didn't want to be embarrassed. Hopefully, the woman he was to marry wouldn't be critical. Or expect multiple forks and spoons at each meal, laid out in a particular way. There was little she liked less than being made to feel foolish.

Even worse was the idea that when his intended did arrive, that maybe she wouldn't find Elaine suitable to be a housekeeper. Surely, she must be used to the best, and Elaine felt as though she were far from that. She was trying, that was all she could do, but she hadn't had proper training to run a house.

But then that led to another thought. Once Melanie was here...if she didn't dismiss her on the spot, what would it be like? Elaine walked toward the books and picked one up, studying the illustration on the cover of a woman holding a man's hand, each of them gazing at the other as though they were the only two in existence.

Elaine traced the image with one finger. Was this what it felt like to be loved? To have someone look at you like you were precious? Like you mattered more than anything?

Her mind flashed unbidden to Oliver—to the way he'd looked at her this morning when he'd caught her, his face so close, his eyes dark and unreadable. For one moment, she'd thought... but no. He'd been startled, that was all.

Concerned she might be hurt. There was nothing more to it.

She set the book down quickly, as though she had no business touching it. But the thought that had been coming frequently emerged again. Could she...could she bear the image of seeing Oliver and Melanie together?

It sounded like perhaps things were a little strained between them, but they'd make the best of it, and Elaine was sure that the initial difficulty they had would vanish once Melanie got used to Cottonwood Falls. So, where did that leave her?

Could she handle seeing them together every day? Their glances of affection toward each other? Embraces? Kisses?

Elaine's chest grew tight at the thought. She wasn't sure that she could. She also had no business even thinking such a thing! It was really none of her business how their relationship was. Besides, Oliver had been nothing but kind to her, upfront that he had someone he'd intended to marry, and here she was letting thoughts of him distract her. It was sinful, and she was ashamed of herself.

She wished she could remember what it was called—she'd read about it once. That feeling someone had when they were helped or rescued by another. An immense gratitude that could lead to confusing feelings. That was all this was. She had no business letting her imagination run away with her.

Except... it wasn't just gratitude, was it? Yes, he'd rescued her from Mr. Smith, and he'd also given her a job. She was grateful for those things. But that...that was a different feeling. What she was experiencing now was something else entirely. Something dangerous. Something that would only lead to heartbreak.

She had to leave. As soon as Melanie arrived and was settled, Elaine would find another position. It was the only way to protect herself—and to protect what little honor she had left.

But she also didn't want to leave. Didn't want to worry that maybe he wasn't eating or looking after himself. Being looked after.

Elaine didn't know what to do, and the agonizing pain was almost unbearable.

"I've got a basketful for you," the store clerk said, drawing Elaine's attention toward her. "I do have to order things. I'll get them as quickly as possible, but you know how it is. It can take a while."

"I'll explain that," Elaine said. "Thank you. Can you please add these pans and the baking tins as well to his account?"

"Of course. And I'll have the delivery boy bring it all over in an hour," the woman said. "May I keep the list?"

Elaine nodded, said goodbye, and walked outside. To her surprise, the seamstress was just inside of her shop door, and waved her over. She hurried toward her, and asked, "Did you need me?"

"Yes. I have Mr. Mason's shirts," the woman answered. "Your dresses are next."

"There is no rush on mine," Elaine assured her, "but he will be thrilled to have these."

"Let me just get them," Sally said.

Elaine followed her into the shop and waited while Sally went into the back room. Absently, she reached for her locket and ran a finger over it.

As Sally returned, she froze, her eyes fixed on Elaine's throat. "That locket at your throat..."

Elaine's fingers instantly went to it. "Yes? Well, half of one, anyway."

Sally's face grew pale. "H-half?" she whispered, not expounding on whatever it was it sounded like she was going to ask.

"Yes. The orphanage said that's all there was. Just the chain and half, the portrait side empty," Elaine answered.

"Well, it's still a lovely necklace," Sally said, her voice strained.

"Thank you. It was my mother's. The only thing I have of hers."

"May I see it?" Sally asked, and something in her tone made Elaine uneasy. But she lifted the chain slightly so the older woman could look.

Sally stared at it for a long moment, her face pale. "It's beautiful," she whispered finally, then turned away quickly. She handed Elaine the shirts, and said, "I will send a bill. Goodbye."

She hurried into the back room, letting out what sounded like a sob, and Elaine stood frozen for a moment, confused and hurt. Why was it the woman seemed upset each time they spoke? Was it truly because she was an orphan? Did Sally think she was trying to cause trouble? Why did she ask about her locket?

Elaine clutched Oliver's shirts to her chest and stepped outside, blinking against the sudden brightness she told herself, not the tears that were threatening her. Everyone assumed the worst of orphans. Even kind-seeming women like Sally. Maybe Oliver's fiancée would think the same. She'd already had concerns over the situation. Maybe Elaine should leave before Melanie arrived and made her feel even smaller than she already did.

But the thought of leaving—of never seeing Oliver again—made her chest tighten so painfully she had to stop walking and catch her breath.

What had she done? How had she let herself care this much about someone she could never have? She was a fool.

Chapter 12

"Oliver?"

He looked up from the column of numbers he'd been reworking and rubbed at his eyes. "Oh! Elaine!"

She set a tray down on the side of his desk. "I brought you something for lunch when you didn't come into the kitchen."

"Lunch? Is it that time already?" Oliver asked, reaching for his pocket watch.

"No, it's past time," Elaine said with a laugh. "But you've been in here all day. I was getting concerned."

He glanced at her face in time to see some hesitation on it. "Thank you," he told her. "I've been trying to get these books for the seamstress sorted. Do you know, when she dropped them off yesterday for me to look over, I thought it would be a simple job. I wasn't really sure why she'd want to hire me."

"I sense the word 'but' coming," Elaine said.

"You do indeed," he told her. "But, I think..." He stopped. He didn't want to speak poorly of anyone, especially a client, so how to say this?

Elaine's eyes flickered toward the row of numbers before him in neat but inaccurate rows. "I wonder if she doesn't have much schooling," she said. "Or else if she has that thing like another girl did in the orphanage, where she sees letters and numbers mixed up."

"It is one of those," Oliver agreed. "However, I am working through it. I think she will be relieved with the end results, and that is that she is more profitable than she realizes."

Elaine clasped her hands before her. "That's wonderful! I hope to get my dresses from her soon. She is a very talented woman. Surely, that news from you will make her very happy."

The smile dropped as the sunshine left Elaine's eyes, almost as if a cloud had passed over her face. "What's wrong?" Oliver asked. "You became quite...pensive."

She drew in a deep breath, not meeting his eyes as she fiddled with moving the tray closer to him. "It's nothing really. Just...every time I go there, she asks me questions about myself, and it seems to, I don't know... I get this impression that she doesn't care for me."

"That can't be right," Oliver said. "Perhaps she was just reminded of another thought?"

"It could be," Elaine agreed. "I am sure I've done nothing to upset her."

"You could never do anything to upset anyone," Oliver told Elaine, standing and moving closer to her. "You are one of the kindest and sweetest women I know. Quite possibly the most."

Her cheeks burned a crimson, and Elaine shyly met his gaze. "Thank you."

Oliver found himself almost lost in her eyes. He wished he could stay there, but someone knocked at the door, startling them both.

"I'll get it," Elaine said, her skirt gently swishing as she left the room.

Oliver groaned, running his fingers through his hair. It was terrible timing, the door, but it was also likely for the best. While he had no idea what he was about to say or do, it wouldn't have been right.

"You've an urgent telegraph message," Elaine said as she walked into his study quickly.

"I hope nothing is wrong with one of my parents," Oliver said. "I can't think who else would send such a thing." He accepted the envelope and tore it open, his fingers shaking slightly. Was one of them in a health crisis? His father had recently had a fall off a horse and had broken his leg. Had that—

"Oh. It's from Melanie," Oliver said, simultaneously relieved and now tense. "It simply says 'arriving tomorrow.'"

"Oh! I'd best hurry to get her room ready," Elaine said. "Unless...unless you are marrying when she arrives tomorrow and she'll stay in yours?"

She was back to not meeting his eyes. Oliver searched his mind as to why that could be, completely dismissing the hope that it was because she didn't want him to marry. That couldn't be it. Elaine was obviously not attracted to him, nor should she be. She was a good woman. Steady, confident in what she did. Honest in all her doings. Beautiful...

He cleared his throat when he realized Elaine was now staring at him. "Ah, no, we are not marrying right away. Melanie isn't sure when her parents will arrive. As she will have her maid, she felt quite safe being here with a chaperone until it's arranged."

Elaine nodded. "I'll go get their room ready. But, Oliver?"

"Yes?"

She was partway to the door and looked over her shoulder. "Please eat your lunch. I worry that you'll forget."

He glanced down at the tray, almost surprised to see it. That's right, she had brought that in. Oliver chuckled. "You know me well," he said.

She just gave that sweet soft laugh he found he adored and left, gently closing the door behind her.

Oliver glanced at the numbers he'd been working, and then at the tray. He wanted to get this done, but eating did sound good right now. He sat, pulling the meal toward him. There were soft slices of bread, some cheese and a cut apple, along with some cold ham. He assembled a sandwich and took a bite, suddenly ravenous.

How was it that Elaine did know him so well? It must be because she was so proficient at her job. That was all. He refused to think that it was because she cared for him outside of her position.

There was a knock at the door again, loud, long, and rapid. The person sounded quite aggravated. With a frown, Oliver rose to answer it himself. He met Elaine hurriedly coming from the kitchen, wiping her hands on her apron. "I'm sorry," she said, "I—"

"Don't apologize," he told her. "Whoever this is, should be patient." He opened the door, and then stilled.

"Hello, Ollie," Melanie said, surrounded by trunks and bags and far more than he thought could fit in his home. She wore an oversized hat he assumed was the latest fashion, and a dress that looked far too frilly for travel.

A young woman stood behind her, dressed in a simple gray dress, her hair in a fancy braid, and was glancing around disapprovingly. She must be her maid, he thought to himself.

"Melanie!" he said, scrambling to put his thoughts in order. "I thought...that is to say, your message said tomorrow."

"It is tomorrow," she said, "so I suppose someone made a mistake. Aren't you going to let me inside?"

"Yes, of course," he said, backing up and opening the door wider. He could see Elaine inching toward the kitchen, and decided not to draw attention to her. That would happen soon enough. "Let me help with your bags."

Almost an hour later, all of Melanie's bags, and those of her maid, Lucy, were squeezed into the room the two would share until Melanie married him. Her parents would be arriving about a week after her, she told him.

"Show me around," Melanie said once the last bag was in her room. "Where is the rest of the house?"

Oliver froze. "This...this is the entirety," he told her. "Three rooms up top, one for myself, one for the housekeeper, and one for you."

She let out a sigh, then said, "At least show me my sitting room."

"There is just one," Oliver said, leading the way down the stairs. "But you can decorate it however you like." He showed her the sitting room, not missing how her arms folded over her chest as she looked it over, then he showed his study, and walked toward the kitchen.

"I think the housekeeper is in the kitchen," he told her. "Since the house isn't very large, Elaine is usually in there if she's not doing a chore or errand."

"Elaine?" Melanie asked, her eyebrows shooting up. "You call your housekeeper by her Christian name?"

"Ah, well." Oliver stopped outside the kitchen door. Finally, he shrugged. "I never thought too much about it."

Melanie walked past him, and Oliver hurried to follow her. Elaine was just pulling a cake out of the oven. Once she'd set it on the counter, she pushed back a loose tendril of hair, and smiled. "Hello. I'm Elaine. You must be Melanie."

There was a long moment of silence. Too long. Melanie finally answered, "Yes. However, I admit to being shocked. Things must be quite relaxed here, for the help to be speaking to their future employer with such familiarity. I suppose if that's how it must be?"

A knock sounded at the door, and Oliver felt relief wash over him. The tension in the air right now was too great. Melanie followed him to the front, where he opened it, grateful to see Edward standing there.

"Cousin!" Edward said cheerfully. "And you must be Melanie."

"I am," his bride-to-be said, inclining her head. "I've heard much about you, Dr. Mason."

"Edward is fine," he told her. "Out here, we are quite relaxed in things."

"So I see," Melanie answered, her voice slightly disapproving. "Oliver calls his housekeeper by her given name, as you called me by mine."

"Caroline and I would like to have you over for dinner Thursday evening," Edward said, not replying to Melanie's obvious jab.

"That sounds wonderful. We'd be delighted," Oliver answered.

"I've got to run, on my way to see a patient. But come about six?" Edward waved a hand and then strode quickly toward a wagon, where his doctor's bag sat upon the seat.

"I do hope the dinner won't be unbearably dull," Melanie said as she walked toward the stairs.

"Why do you think it would be?" Oliver asked. "Edward and his wife are good people, and able to converse well."

"They are also doctors. We will have nothing in common," Melanie answered, her brows rising even further. "I'm getting a terrible feeling about this entire situation. Really, Ollie, this is where you expect me to live the rest of my days?"

Oliver wasn't sure what to say. Embarrassment and anger warred with confusion and hurt. He stood there trying to think over the words that were wanting to free themselves as Melanie walked up the stairs. A slight movement caught his eye, and he saw Elaine in the kitchen.

The look of sympathy on her face was almost unbearable. She'd heard everything. Heard Melanie's disdain, her dismissal of his home, his choices, his life. And somehow, having Elaine witness it made the humiliation a thousand times worse.

He turned away, unable to face her, and hurried to his study before he did something foolish. Like go to her. Like forget, for one dangerous moment, that he had no right to want her sympathy.

Chapter 13

"Are these the only choices you have for tea?" Lucy asked, then pressed her lips together. "Just these three?"

"Yes," Elaine said, giving the same answer as she had the last few days. "This is the one requested by Melanie—"

"Miss Charles," Lucy corrected.

Elaine ignored her. "And these are the other two we have. Peppermint and chamomile. If you'd like me to get something else from the store, I will."

That was something else she'd said the last few days, but neither Melanie nor her maid had taken her up on the offer.

"We will make do," Lucy said with a sigh. "Back home, there were at least a dozen to choose from."

"How very nice," Elaine replied, gritting her teeth.

"It was. Far nicer than this place is," Lucy said. "I really don't know how she'll survive in such a rugged town. Miss Charles is used to only the best."

Blowing out a breath, Elaine turned back to the breakfast dishes she was washing. That twelve dollars a week was starting to feel too little for the aggravation she sensed was to come from Oliver's future wife and her maid. Was that how it was with people back East? They had so much more to choose from, that a choice between three teas was too scanty?

It had been hard to be polite. Melanie and Lucy reminded her of some of the spoiled guests there had been at the hotel, so she just thought of them that way and managed. But it was the fact that they seemed to always be underfoot!

Melanie had been bored. She moped about and paced, and didn't want to go for walks because of how dusty it was. Oliver had told her it was still cleaner than the streets of Boston, but she'd had a ready answer for that as well, though Elaine hadn't heard it.

The kitchen door opened, and Elaine braced herself to see Lucy again, but instead of Lucy was Oliver, hands in his pockets and shoulders hunched slightly.

Her heart sank. Since Melanie's arrival, the Oliver she'd known had slowly vanished. He hadn't smiled, hadn't laughed, had just stayed in his study, working, when he wasn't trying his best to entertain his fiancée. The change in him was like watching a light go out. Where he'd been warm and open, now he was guarded.

And it was breaking her heart to watch. She wanted to shake Melanie and demand, "Don't you see what you're doing to him? Don't you care?" But of course she couldn't. Melanie was his chosen one. Elaine was just the housekeeper. All she could do was take care of him in this way.

"Can I get you anything?" Elaine asked, hoping he'd say yes and she could help in some way.

His eyes met hers, and his mouth opened briefly before it snapped shut, and he shook his head. She wondered what he had considered saying.

"No, just...I just..." His eyes darted around the room. "A drink. I was thirsty."

Elaine nodded, and set to filling a cup with some water for him, fresh from the spring that morning.

"Thank you," Oliver said, as he took it from her.

Their eyes locked, and Elaine sensed he was struggling with wanting to say something, but he didn't. "Are you..." She stopped and tried again. "Is there anything else I can get you?"

"I—"

"Ollie! Where are you?" Melanie's voice came from the hallway, and Elaine could have sworn she saw him flinch.

The door burst open, and Melanie stood there, hands on her hips. "I've been looking for you," she said. "I'm bored. Are you done with those silly numbers now? Take me to the general store. I want to do something interesting before we go to dinner with your cousin and his wife. I also should get her a gift. We might be in this little backwards town, but I can still uphold the proper societal expectations."

Oliver's eyes flicked toward her, and he nodded. "Of course. Let me get my hat."

He followed her out, and if he looked over his shoulder, Elaine didn't know. She was too busy squeezing her hands into fists as she picked up the kitchen rag to wipe at the counter.

How could she speak to him that way? Oliver was a kind person, but he was also a busy one! He had to work; this was his job. He wasn't her plaything to just order about. Nor was he happy. That much was obvious.

And she called him 'Ollie' with such casual ownership, as though he were a possession rather than a person. As though she had the right to command him, to interrupt him, to dismiss his work as 'silly.'

Elaine's stomach churned. She had no claim to Oliver, no right to be angry on his behalf, but hearing Melanie treat him so carelessly made something fierce and protective rise in her chest.

Not for the first time since she'd seen Melanie, Elaine wondered what kind of marriage the two would have. Melanie was pretty, there was no mistaking that. She was downright beautiful, with soft brown hair, large green eyes, and a tall woman, with a slim, elegant figure. It was obvious she'd be the most attractive person in town.

But Elaine wasn't sure that her insides matched her outsides. Melanie wasn't cruel, but she seemed careless, spoiled, and impatient. How in the world had Oliver fallen in love with her? The loneliness she felt at times made Elaine miss Lizzie all the more.

Last night, she'd written a letter to Lizzie. She'd gotten one from her a few days ago, with an address of where Elaine could reply for the next month. It had made her happy to hear all of her friend's news, and how her new job was going.

Elaine had given her an abbreviated description of her new job, and how she'd chosen that instead of a wedding. She'd mentioned Melanie, and admitted her struggle internally to accept her role, wondering on page if maybe she wasn't suited for this job after all.

What Elaine hadn't said, however, was that it wasn't because of the tasks or even Melanie that made her wonder that. It was because of the heartache she felt, seeing how miserable Oliver looked, and that feeling she had of how he deserved better. He deserved someone who cared for him.

And she wanted that person to be her.

The realization didn't surprise her anymore—she'd been trying not to admit it for some time now. But saying it, even in her own mind, felt like a confession of the worst kind. Oliver was a promised man. And here was Elaine, the housekeeper, coveting what belonged to another woman. She hated herself for it. Hated that she couldn't stop thinking about him, couldn't stop wishing Melanie would disappear and leave them to the quiet life they'd had before. It was sinful. Wrong.

And yet… she couldn't make herself stop feeling it.

"Elaine?"

She gasped and spun, startled as Oliver stood behind her.

"Are you okay?" he asked, concern on his face.

"Fine, fine, you just surprised me is all," she said, laughing nervously. "I was woolgathering."

He grinned at her, the first she'd seen in days. "I do that too. I just wanted to remind you that you don't need to worry about dinner, but for yourself and Lucy. We're eating with Edward and Caroline tonight."

Elaine nodded. "I remember, but thank you. I'm just making something simple for Lucy, and since tonight is my last night at the boardinghouse, eating there with Mrs. Harper."

He nodded, and started toward the door, then paused, looking over his shoulder. "I'll be glad to have you here all the time," he said.

"Ollie!" an impatient voice called.

His shoulders dropped, and he pushed through the door wordlessly.

Elaine pressed her hands to her chest. What had he meant? Was he...

"Stop," she told herself firmly in a whisper. "Don't make things up. There's no way that Oliver could mean anything more than he's glad you are here, as a housekeeper."

It didn't matter that there was the slightest spark she hoped meant otherwise.

Chapter 14

As dessert was brought to them, by Edward and Caroline's housekeeper, Oliver hoped his stomach settled enough to eat it. Mounds of whipped cream were piled high on a sponge cake and covered in freshly picked blueberries. At any other moment, his mouth would have been watering and he'd have been eager to dip his fork into the treat, but dinner had not been going so well.

At first, Melanie had been polite, even if short with her answers, clearly disinterested in getting to know his cousin and his wife. But as the soup turned into the main meal, she'd picked at it with obvious disdain, not seeming to like the pork chop and green beans and mashed potatoes. Her fork had poked and prodded, and she'd hardly eaten a bite.

It wasn't because the food wasn't tasty. It was. Edward's housekeeper was a wonderful cook. It was just obvious to everyone that Melanie didn't want to be there, no matter how they tried to make her feel welcome.

"There's a town about an hour or so away by wagon," Caroline said. "Perhaps we ladies could go for a shopping day."

"What's the point?" Melanie asked. "The stores will likely be similar to those here. Small, with a limited selection and nothing that's interesting or of the latest fashion."

Oliver was about to say something when Caroline shrugged. "We do our best, but out here, practicality rules before fancies. Oliver, tell me, did Mrs. Lapstick stop by with her ledgers for you to look at?"

"Not yet," he said, raising his head to meet her eyes. "But I thank you for mentioning me to her."

Edward gave him a warm smile. "A good accountant is something this town has needed for a good number of years. I'm glad you're here."

"For now," Melanie said. "But I don't see how one could actually make a life here. It's so...so..." She waved a hand around and then resumed poking at the plate before her.

Oliver had had quite enough. "I think we must leave shortly," he said, trying to push remorse into his voice. "I have a client's books I need to finish by tomorrow afternoon."

"Of course," Edward said cheerfully, though Oliver was sure his cousin knew exactly why he'd said that. "We won't keep you. There will be plenty more opportunities to have dinner together. So, let's enjoy our desserts and say goodnight."

A half hour later, he and Melanie were saying their farewells and leaving. They walked back to his home, and Oliver fought to keep his voice calm as he said, "I am sorry you didn't enjoy the evening."

Melanie didn't answer. That was probably a good thing. He wasn't sure he could have kept his temper if she'd criticized anything else. As they approached the house, he could see a light on in the front window, and a figure moving within. He wondered if it was Lucy or whether it was Elaine.

"Is Lucy settling in?" Oliver asked, curious about the maid. She stayed close to Melanie, but rarely spoke.

"Who could settle in here?" Melanie asked.

"A lot of people have," Oliver said with a frown. "I am one of them."

"Really, I think you are wasted here," Melanie told him, resting a hand on his arm. "You could be doing the accounting for large companies. For businessmen, for millionaires. Yet, you are here working for shoemakers."

The disdain in her voice was obvious, but Oliver tamped down his upset. "Shoemakers are businessmen," he answered. "And work is work."

"Don't you want more?" Melanie asked, pausing just before the door. "Don't you want to live and enjoy your life?"

Oliver thought for a moment, then said, "But I do. In fact, I enjoy it more here than I ever did in Boston. There's room to breathe. Things are clean. The sunsets and sunrises are glorious. The people here are good, and kind, and honest. This is a place where a man can feel rested, in body and soul."

She searched his face, and Oliver saw something flicker in her eyes. He wasn't sure what it was. Sadness? It was too dark to tell, and she didn't answer, but walked inside the house.

Lucy greeted her immediately, and they went up the stairs. Oliver stood watching her, wondering what had been going through Melanie's mind just a moment before. How could he help her to see what he saw? Love the things that he loved about Cottonwood Falls?

He rubbed at his eyes. He did actually need to work a little, but first, maybe he could find something light to take back to his study, in case he was there for a while.

Oliver made his way to the kitchen. Elaine was just closing a cupboard door and when she saw him smiled. "You're back. How was dinner?" she asked.

"The meal was good," he told her truthfully.

"Hopefully, the conversation was as well," she answered. "But you are home far earlier than I would have thought."

There was no answer he could give her that wouldn't seem critical. So, he just shrugged. Even that motion felt difficult. His shoulders, his chest, all of him had felt as though it was so heavy as of late. It nearly crushed him.

"I need to work for a little," Oliver said. "I thought I might make a snack and take it with me."

"I'll make you one," Elaine said, and started to bustle around.

"You don't have to," he told her.

"I want to." Elaine turned and met his eyes, and Oliver found something within him ease slightly. He had no idea why.

"Thank you," he said quietly.

She nodded, turned away, then busied herself with the kettle.

"If...if being here is extra stress for you," Oliver said, unsure why he was suddenly offering, "you don't have to stay. I can help you find another place."

"Why would I want to go elsewhere?" Elaine asked. She raised an eyebrow. "Is it you or Melanie don't like how I do my job?"

"That's not it at all," he hastened to assure her. "It's because of..."

He stopped. He couldn't say it. How terrible it would sound. But it seemed as if Elaine understood, as she cocked her head slightly to one side, and said, "It's all right. People are..." She thought for a moment, then finished, "People-y at times. But I like my job. I love being here. I love helping you. Taking care of you."

A charge filled the air without warning. Oliver found himself gazing into Elaine's eyes, helpless to look away. There was so much that he found himself wanting to say. At the same time, he knew that he shouldn't. He had Melanie. Was going to marry Melanie. But she never made him feel this way. Loved and wanted and taken care of and special.

Melanie had never once asked if he'd eaten. Had never worried about him working too long. Had never looked at him the way Elaine was looking at him now—with tenderness and concern and something else he didn't dare name.

Oliver found himself reaching for Elaine, his hand trembling slightly as he whispered her name. "Elaine..."

She took his hand, squeezed it gently, and then footsteps in the hallway made her drop it. "Tea or coffee?" she asked, turning away again.

"T-tea," Oliver said.

The kitchen door opened, and Lucy stood, her lips pressed in a line. "Since you are making a tray, my mistress would also like one. I'll take it to her."

"Of course," Elaine said. She shook her head slightly at Oliver, who'd been about to interrupt and tell Lucy that she could very well make one herself. He thought better of it then. Elaine might not like anyone poking about in her kitchen.

A moment later, Elaine had the trays prepared, and Oliver took his to his study, leaving the kitchen at the same time as Lucy. Before he shut his door, he turned to see Elaine walking up the stairs, a lamp to light her way in one hand.

"I'm a fool," he whispered.

It was true. He was. He had a woman he was to marry, someone he should have loved. She loved him, didn't she? Yet, he'd almost told Elaine the singular thought that kept going around in his head.

That somehow, he wasn't sure when, he'd found himself drawn to her. Felt something for her.

"I'm worse than a fool," he growled, glaring down at the tray. "She's not even a possibility. Not a choice. My life is set, the plan made and lined up, like the numbers in this ledger. Every second spent thinking about Elaine is a betrayal of the woman who will bear my name."

He sat heavily at his desk, dropping his head into his hands. He hadn't expected this when he'd asked Melanie to marry him, nor when he'd moved here, nor when he'd hired Elaine. What a mess he found himself in. Filled with self loathing and despair, and love for a woman he couldn't have. He needed to try harder with Melanie. They used to laugh together. Smile, feel at ease. He wished things hadn't changed, but they had the moment he'd asked her to marry him, and there was no help for it. But he could stop thinking about Elaine. He had to try.

"I am the worst of men," Oliver whispered.

Chapter 15

It had been difficult to sleep the night before, and that made the afternoon chores all the more exhausting. Oliver's face, tortured and as though he'd wanted to say more to her, had stayed with her all night long. Elaine told herself not to read into things.

He was not only a gentleman with an important job, he was also from a higher class than she was. She was on her own, a woman who needed to make her own way. No matter what, the thing she was feeling when around him couldn't exist.

Elaine had always been conscious of class differences. How could she avoid them, growing up in an orphanage? She had been reminded daily of how little she and the others mattered, hence their being there, but had used that to drive herself toward getting as good of an education as possible. The orphanage did have teachers, many of them former orphans themselves, who stressed the importance of being educated and looking after oneself. That was something Elaine had taken to heart.

When she started working at the hotel, that was the first time she'd been surrounded by such a divide and it had been almost overwhelming at first. There were so many guests who were wealthy, they treated her and the other staff as though they were invisible, unless they wanted something. Then, they were impatient, critical, and looked down their noses.

While she'd been seeking work after the hotel burned down, Elaine had felt that same lacking they'd supposed in her. Coming here to Cottonwood Falls was the first time she'd ever felt judged on her own merits.

Well, at least by most of the townsfolk. The seamstress seemed...odd. But Elaine knew that there was always someone, somewhere, who would look down on her. At least Oliver didn't. From the first moment they'd met, he'd treated her with respect. Kindness. As though she mattered—not because of what she could do for him, but simply because she existed.

No one had ever made her feel that way before. No one had ever looked at her the way he did, with warmth in his eyes and genuine interest in what she had to say. It was one of the many reasons she'd fallen in love with him, though she tried to deny that thought. And it was one of the many reasons loving him hurt so much.

It was so hard not to think about Oliver. Losing herself in work helped, but there was only so much to be done around here. Truthfully, everything had been done this morning, which gave Elaine no excuse to avoid going to the seamstress for her final approval on her new dresses.

A note had arrived yesterday, asking her to come at her earliest convenience. While Elaine was excited to have the new dresses, she also felt anxious about the interaction she'd be having with the woman. Hopefully, today there wouldn't be any problems. She really didn't want to spoil something so lovely as having new dresses by the woman looking down on her.

With a last look around the kitchen, Elaine removed her apron, smoothed down her hair and dress, and set out. It was windy today, and appeared that a storm might be rolling in, based on the dark clouds that were filling the sky, blotting out all of the sunshine that had been there recently.

Though she wasn't superstitious, Elaine hoped very much that this wasn't some sort of a terrible omen.

When she arrived at the seamstress's shop, she paused, letting her eyes take in the new dresses hung there, then let herself inside.

The seamstress glanced up, and smiled. That made Elaine feel slightly better. Perhaps the woman had been under some sort of stress about other things during their previous interactions, and it had bled into their conversation.

"Hello," Elaine said. "I received your note. I'm most looking forward to seeing the dresses."

"I think you'll like them," Sally said, gesturing for Elaine to follow her to the back room. She called over her shoulder, "The fabrics will look perfect on you."

"I can't wait," Elaine said, unable to hide her eagerness.

Elaine removed her work dress, and shimmied into the first Sally offered her. She was led to several small mirrors the woman had placed in a row, so that she could see nearly the entirety of herself.

Sally had been right. It was perfect. The soft color made her skin nearly glow, the cut was superb, and Elaine could tell right away that she'd be able to move about easily, and the fabric would withstand many washings. The stitching was so fine, and Elaine was sure that she'd never have another dress she loved as much as this one. Unbidden, tears sprang to her eyes.

She looked toward the seamstress, who was watching her, an anxious look on her face. "What do you think? Is something wrong? I can't tell from your expression."

"No, it's perfect," Elaine said, clasping her hands to her chest, before smoothing them down the bodice and waist. "It's just so lovely. I never imagined I'd have something like this of my own. It's...it's overwhelming." The final word came out a sob, and embarrassment filled her at her emotional outburst.

Elaine did a half turn, staring into the mirror, and for a moment—just a fleeting, foolish moment—she let herself imagine the first time Oliver would see her in it. Would his eyes widen? Would he smile that soft smile he sometimes gave her? Would he think she looked... pretty? The fantasy was dangerous and she pushed it away, but not before her heart ached with something she couldn't identify.

As Elaine frantically wiped at her eyes, she was surprised to see the seamstress also sniffling. "Let's try them all," the woman said, bringing over the next dress.

Elaine tried on each, exclaiming over the dresses as she ran her hands over the lengths. Sally looked so pleased, her cheeks were pink, though her eyes still wore some of that sadness she seemed to carry.

As she paid her balance, Elaine said, "I appreciate both the care you put into these, and also the speed with which you got them to me."

"It was my pleasure," Sally said. "I am so pleased you came to me."

"I am too," Elaine said, collecting her dresses that were now wrapped in brown paper.

"May I ask a question..." Sally hesitated. "About your necklace?"

Elaine's fingers wrapped around it, instinctively, the metal warm from being against her skin. She nodded, and waited to hear the question.

"Are there any markings on the backside?" Sally asked.

"No," Elaine said, then her eyebrows furrowed. "I have studied it many times and never seen one."

"I see." The words came out as a whisper, then the seamstress nodded, swallowing visibly.

Her door opened just then and two women walked in. There was almost relief on her face as she greeted them.

"Thank you again," Elaine said, taking her dresses and leaving.

The question had been very odd, but at least this time, there hadn't been that feeling she'd had before, of being suspect of something. While she'd been trying on the dresses, in fact, at the final dress, the seamstress had looked happy, her eyes shining and the sorrow that had always filled them temporarily gone.

That is, until the question of the locket. But even then, she'd looked more thoughtful. Tense.

The entire situation was odd, but Elaine decided to think nothing more about it. People would always be curious about an orphan, about the type of person who could be abandoned. No matter she'd been an infant. The questions were something she was used to, and had been answering her entire life. At first, it had bothered her. Now, it was nothing more than just a question.

There had been a day, a moment, back when she'd been so very young, when Elaine had thought she might be adopted. But it hadn't happened. How different her life might be than it was right now, had she been taken for another's child.

Elaine glanced up at the sky. While it was dark out, the rain had held. She was glad of that. She was anxious to get her dresses put away and get dinner started.

When she let herself inside, the house was quiet. With a little difficulty that she didn't mind in the least from her full arms, Elaine went to her room, unwrapped her dresses one by one, and hung them up.

She allowed herself a moment to admire them. Tonight, she'd have to think about which of them she'd wear tomorrow! It felt extravagant getting so many at once, but only this morning, she'd discovered another thin spot, threatening to tear on the dress she wore. These dresses would last her for a long time, and would be a joy to wear.

As she walked back to the kitchen, Elaine found her fingers around her locket again. They rubbed against every familiar line and bump. All of Sally's questions about her locket had made her start to wonder something.

What if the woman with the other half of the locket was still out there? Or, what if...what if the locket had been split into two because she had a sister? Her chest caught in excitement, and she decided to write to the orphanage and ask. While they'd have likely told her if that was the case, maybe she'd had a sister who hadn't survived. It felt important just to know, good news or bad, that she had family, somewhere, or had had family.

The thought was both exciting and also filled her with a sudden sadness. Maybe she shouldn't write. Maybe she shouldn't have even thought about it. She'd been alone for so many years, she was used to it. New information wouldn't change things.

But what if she wasn't alone? The tiny hope spoke, flickering in her mind and torturing her with confusion. All her life, she'd wanted to belong somewhere. To someone. To have a place where she fit, where she was wanted. She'd thought maybe she'd found that here, in this house, with Oliver. But that had been a foolish dream. He belonged to someone else. Melanie would soon be taking her rightful place. Perhaps finding family—real family, blood family—was the belonging she was meant to have after all.

Elaine let out a deep sigh. Too many questions, so much unknowing, and all of it brought a pain to her heart. It was best to stop. Besides, there was no time to think of such things. She needed to start dinner. She reached for her apron and began to tie the long strings about her waist.

A shout filled the house, startling her. Before she'd fully comprehended what was happening, Elaine went running toward it.

Oliver's voice cried out again, filled with panic.

Chapter 16

"I can't," Oliver said to Melanie. "I've taken you out every night this week. I've also taken you out every lunch, and for long strolls through town, and rides in a rented carriage, but I've got to get this done. I just have to."

"Oh, you are no fun at all," Melanie said with a pout. She stood and tossed her book aside. She'd been reading in his study, which he hadn't minded, but about a half hour ago, when Melanie had gotten restless and started to sigh and move around, it had become distracting. A dangerous thing, when he needed to concentrate on numbers.

"Please, Ollie. You don't realize just how much I'm suffering here." She wrapped her arms around his right arm as she stood at the side of his chair. "If I were back home, I'd have something enjoyable to do."

"You are home," Oliver reminded her. "Well, you will be as soon as we are married, that is."

She didn't answer, just pouted. "You can do it later. It's just silly rows of numbers you are calculating. Take me now."

"It's more than that," Oliver said defensively. "And this is my job, Melanie. What provides the roof over our heads. Can't you amuse yourself for a while? Perhaps you and Lucy can go out."

"She's got a headache," Melanie said, straightening. She paced around the room. "There's so much dust, it's terrible for her sinuses. This town isn't any fun. You aren't any fun. I hate it here."

Oliver closed his eyes for a moment. "I'm sorry it's been so different from what you'd expected," he told her.

"Then help me find ways to enjoy myself," Melanie said. She walked toward him and sat on the edge of his desk. "Take me out. Right now. We can go eat at the diner. Maybe they've got strawberry pie. That at least is nice."

She leaned in closely, then let out a yelp as the glass of water sitting on his desk tipped from her movement.

With a shout he hardly recognized pulled from him, Oliver jumped up, frantically grabbing at the ledger sheets before him, but it was too late. The rows and columns were soaked, and the ink started to bleed. It was a blurry mess. He stood in shock at the loss of hours of work, and the realization it would be hours and hours more to right it.

"I'm sorry," Melanie said, genuine anguish on her face for a moment. Then it vanished as quickly as he recognized it. Her face grew hopeful. "That must be a sign. You must take me out."

"What? How can you think that?" Oliver said in disbelief, as he mopped at the top of his desk with his handkerchief. All he could do now was to try and prevent his desk from damage. It was too late for the ledger.

"If we go now, you'll have loads of time to work on it this evening," Melanie said, wrapping her arms around his neck. "You'll be refreshed, and it will go much faster. And," she added, fluttering her eyelashes, "I'll leave you be the moment we get back so you can work on it."

Oliver hesitated, glancing between the soggy sheets and Melanie. Would she? If she did, and they just had dinner, he'd be able to recopy the numbers, work them out, and be sure the ledger for his client was correct and ready on time.

"You promise?" he asked.

"I do," she said, giggling as she tugged him to the door. "Let's go!"

They passed Elaine in the hallway. She'd obviously been coming toward them because of the commotion, but had appeared to stop, likely because she hadn't been called for, and he and Melanie had been talking.

As Elaine's eyes darted between them and toward his study, Oliver stopped, pulling free of Melanie's grasp for a moment. “I’m afraid I had a spill on my desk,” he said. “I…I’m going to take Melanie to the diner and for a short walk. Would you mind wiping the rest for me? Leave the ledger sheets there. I’ll get them on my return. Perhaps they’ll be dry.”

His voice was strained, he knew it was. How could it not be, with the stress he was feeling?

“Of course,” Elaine said. “I’ll take care of it.”

He opened his mouth, wanting to say something more—to thank her properly, to apologize for leaving, to explain—but Melanie tugged impatiently on his arm.

“Ollie! Come on!”

He let himself be pulled away, but glanced back once to see Elaine watching him go, worry playing on her face. He wanted to tell her he was fine. But…was he?

Melanie begged for a stroll first, so they walked through the town, then into the seamstress’s shop, the general store, and along a bank where a partially dried creek ran.

Then, they went to the diner where she lingered over her food, quite oblivious to his impatience and burning desire to get back to his study and resume work. A few times, Melanie seemed as though she wanted to say something more significant than the chatter she’d kept up, but each time she’d hesitated and opened her mouth, nothing came out and she closed it again.

Oliver felt too upset to try and pull whatever it was out of her. It was hard to think about much she said. Not when his mind was consumed with the need to keep working.

Just when they were finally about to leave to go back home, the faint strains of music hit their ears.

"What's happening?" Melanie asked.

"I'm not sure. We can take a quick look," Oliver offered, also curious.

The two walked down the main street of the town, near the end where a small stage had been erected in the time they were at the diner. Several chairs were set on it, with musicians in them tuning their instruments. Others from town took the chairs in the rows before the stage, slowly filling them.

"It looks to be some sort of performance," Melanie said. "Oh, please, Ollie. Let's stay!" She sat in the front row, eyes focused on a woman with a violin.

He hesitated, torn between wanting to please Melanie and keeping his client, but sat next to her. "Just for a little," he told her. "I really must—"

"Yes, yes, I know. You've said it many times," Melanie said impatiently.

Oliver drew a deep breath, trying to remain patient as the first piece began. Several hours passed quickly as the musicians played, a few very talented people in town sang along, and everyone lost themselves in the concert.

Well, everyone it seemed, but him. Oliver watched the musicians but couldn't concentrate on the music. All he could think about was the ruined ledger waiting at home, the hours of work ahead of him.

Stars slowly filled the night sky, but the music continued, the town now lit by lamps and candles. When the final strains had ended, and applause filled the air, Oliver and Melanie had made their way back after several conversations with women asking Melanie about her dress, and the latest fashions back East.

Oliver felt more than impatient. He felt frantic. It must be after ten o'clock! It was too dark to read his pocket watch, but his eyes felt tired, gritty with the desire to sleep.

"Thank you for the lovely evening," Melanie said as he unlocked the door. Her mouth opened, then closed again, much as it had during dinner, and that same hesitation filled her face.

"Is something else wrong?" Oliver asked, only a little ashamed of how his tone sounded. "It's late. Surely you don't still wish to walk around."

Sadness washed over her face. "No, not at all. I just..." Melanie took a deep breath and searched his face. "I just wanted one more enjoyable evening with you. And I've had it. Goodnight, Oliver."

She went up the stairs, and he couldn't help but stare after her, wondering at the strange thing she'd just said, and the fact she'd called him Oliver. That especially felt odd after so many years of calling him Ollie.

Rubbing at his eyes, Oliver went into the kitchen to make himself some coffee as quietly as possibly. It would take hours to work on the ledger, and he prayed he wouldn't fall asleep over it. He'd made a mistake staying out so late, but what more could he have done?

With a sigh, he made his way down toward his study, pausing in the hallway as a flicker of light came from within. Fury burned through him then. She'd promised! Melanie had promised to leave him be to work!

Angrily, he pushed the door open wider, ready to confront her. A righteous anger filled him. He was justified this time in the resentment he felt, and he planned to let her know.

Chapter 17

Elaine hadn't missed the upset expression on Oliver's face when he left with Melanie. Nor how he'd looked at his study with something akin to panic in his eyes.

As she removed the cup and the soggy handkerchief onto a small tray, Elaine winced at the ruined numbers Oliver had been working on. It would take him a good deal of time to redo them, and she knew that Mr. Waterstone needed them by tomorrow morning for a meeting with a banker about a loan. Oliver had promised that he'd be able to complete the short-notice job. But, would he now?

She returned the tray to the kitchen, where she washed the cup and looked out the window. Oliver and Melanie were nowhere to be seen. Lucy had been in her and Melanie's room all day with a headache. A stew was simmering for dinner that night, and rolls were already baked, as was a cobbler. There wasn't much more to do just now.

Elaine picked up her book, intending to read it, when an idea formed. She hesitated, then set the book down. Did she dare? No, it wasn't her place.

She bit her lip, then went outside to sweep the front and saw Oliver and Melanie walking into a store. The anxious expression on his face made her wheel around and go back inside.

Her heart was pounding a little as she walked down the hallway to Oliver's study and glanced at his desk. She studied the ruined papers once more, and then her eyes fell on the original ledger, safe, secure, but inaccurate.

What if she helped him? Would he be upset? This was so important to him. He was...so important to her. She longed to help him, make things easier for him.

Elaine sighed, letting her fingers trail over his desk. Any day, Melanie's parents would arrive, and he and Melanie would marry. It would be official, he'd belong to her. And all those secretive hopes she'd had would be dashed.

Maybe when that time came, she'd leave. She could write Lizzie, tell her to hold all her letters until she knew where she was going to go. Mrs. Harper had talked about a town called Spring Falls that wasn't too far away. She'd also told her about a school for orphans in Hackberry Falls. Perhaps she could seek employment there. Surely, they'd be accepting of one of their own.

While Oliver had never made her feel less than who she was, which she appreciated, how could she stay, watching the man she couldn't stop thinking about with someone else? She hated herself for loving him. She shouldn't. He was spoken for. But, somehow, she still did.

This—helping with the ledgers—would be her gift to him. Perhaps even a goodbye gift.

With a little hesitation, Elaine reached for Oliver's top drawer, where he kept his blank ledger pages. With so many of his clients preferring that he use those to have a backup of their accounts, and ones that were accurate, he had a thick supply of the paper.

Next, she reached for one of the pencils, and, after a moment, settled herself down in his chair. Elaine had watched Oliver many times. First, he'd write the client's name at the top of the sheet, and he'd make the rows, listing out the date and the reason for the financial transaction, then putting the numbers that corresponded into one of the three right columns, the furthest left for when money was taken away, the middle for when it was added, and the far right the current running balance.

Carefully, line by line, Elaine copied out the information about the date and the reason the transaction was made. Then, she penciled in either the deduction or the addition. Slowly, she worked page by page through the thick book, filling row after row.

Her fingers felt cramped, and more than once she had to stop to sharpen the pencil. Shadows fell, and the room darkened. Elaine only stopped to light the lamp. Once, she glanced outside, wondering where Oliver and Melanie could be. Surely, it was getting late.

But stopping to wonder and to seek the time would cause her to waste precious minutes. She wasn't adding the columns, she'd leave that for Oliver, but if she could get everything copied, it would save him hours of work.

Elaine's eyes started to feel gritty as she finished the thirty-second sheet of numbers. As she had with each previously, line by line, she checked that everything was accurate. And hoped that neither Oliver nor Mr. Waterstone would be upset she was doing this part of the task. Mr. Waterstone would never know unless Oliver told him. So that made her feel a little better.

A yawn escaped. Elaine rubbed at her eyes and studied the pages before her. She had three left to copy, and that's what she'd do. Leaving this room before it was done wasn't an option. There was simply no way at all that Oliver could have copied everything, and then added the numbers, in the short time he'd have before Mr. Waterstone arrived at nine the following morning. But if she could finish copying this out, there was a good chance he could add the numbers, and verify the man's current financial numbers were correct so he could get the loan he sought.

Elaine continued to scratch out the rows of dates, words, and numbers. As she finally reached the last page, slowly, she went over it line by line, like she had all of the others. Her eyes felt heavy, and she couldn't help it. She had to rest. She was too tired to stand and go up the stairs.

"Just for a moment," Elaine whispered, "just long enough to get energy to move."

She neatly stacked the papers, then set them to the side, folding her arms on the desktop and resting her head on them. A minute or two was all she needed. Then, she'd rouse herself, write Oliver an apologetic note for touching his desk and papers, and try and get a few hours of sleep before her duties started the next morning.

Her heavy eyes were eager to close, and Elaine found herself in that place between wake and sleep, where one's mind wandered and it was difficult to discern what was real and what was dreamland.

"Elaine?"

"Mmm?" Elaine wasn't sure if she'd really heard her name or not, and was too tired to move, too tired to care.

There was a gentle pressure on her arms, then around her, and she felt as though she were floating, flying through the air. It must be a dream, for there was the faint scent of shaving soap, and ink, and paper, the familiar scent of all the things Oliver was. Warm, safe, kind.

She sighed softly, and turned over, her cheek nestling into her pillow as she pulled the blanket higher around her. There was the softest of brushes against her cheek, and Elaine imagined his lips there and smiled.

It was a wonderful dream, and she hoped she would never wake.

Chapter 18

The anger Oliver had felt turned into surprise when he laid eyes on Elaine, asleep at his desk. He stepped closer, unsure if he should wake her, and hating to, but he needed to get to work. Those numbers wouldn't…write themselves?

His eyes fell on the neatly stacked papers next to Elaine and his breath caught. This! This was why she was here? He picked them up quickly, flipping through the neat rows of numbers, matching each page as quickly as he could to Mr. Waterstone's original ledger.

Elaine had copied everything. It was all there, perfect. Waiting for him to add.

Oliver drew in a shaking breath. This had saved him hours. Had, in truth, saved his job with this client, because there was no way at all he'd have been able to copy and also tally up the numbers. His eyes fell on her again. Sound asleep, a strand of hair across her cheek.

She had to have been working from the time that he had left to take Melanie out. A job like this would take hours; he knew this from experience.

Without thinking, he reached out a finger and gently pushed the hairs from her face. She didn't move. The poor woman. She was likely beyond exhausted. He glanced around, unsure what to do. Should he leave her here while he finished working? It would be better to get her to her room; she'd be far more comfortable.

"Elaine?" he whispered.

"Mmm." Her answer was more a

sigh, and she didn't stir.

Oliver hesitated, then put an arm around her back, and one under her legs, picking her up far easier than he'd have thought. He was both relieved she didn't startle awake and cry out, and surprised that she snuggled into him with another sweet sigh. He studied her a moment, unable to stop the smile on his face as he carried her up the stairs and gently set her into her bed.

The only movement that she made was that of snuggling into her pillow. Oliver pulled the blankets up around her and slipped out of the room, making his way back down the stairs. It had taken a lot not to stop and stare at her, watch and be sure she was fine, that she could somehow sense his gratefulness.

Even still, Oliver knew he had to get started working, and returned to his study, pulling his drink closer, taking a big sip and starting to work. Time passed quickly—too quickly. He stopped only twice. Once to refill the lamp with oil and once to get more to drink.

It wasn't long before the sun started to peak on the horizon. Oliver rubbed at his eyes, but looked back over the final page. He'd done it. And with a few hours to spare. He'd go and lie down, get a little rest before his meeting.

With a yawn, he stood, intending to seek out Elaine if she was awake, and ask her to knock on his door at eight.

But as he walked into the hallway, the woman who came from the opposite direction wasn't Elaine, but Melanie. And her face was one of seriousness.

"Can we talk for a moment?" she asked. "I know you must be exhausted. I promise not to keep you, but what I have to say can't wait. The stage leaves in an hour."

"The stage?" Oliver repeated. He searched his mind. Had she said something about it last night, and he'd simply forgotten, in his worry over Mr. Waterstone's business? Were her parents arriving today? But then why did she say leave?

"Yes." Melanie stood before him, her hands clasped. Without preamble, she continued. "We are not suited, you and I. Not to be anything more than friends. I let others talk me into something that I didn't want. That I knew you didn't want."

"Mel—"

"Let me finish, Ollie. This is already very hard to say." She took a deep breath. "I knew that all along, both before I arrived and after, and that's why I pushed so hard, was so demanding, trying to make you tire of me. That includes last night. The drink...it wasn't an accident."

"That was done on purpose?" Oliver asked, surprised and far too exhausted to be angry. "But why would you do such a thing?"

Melanie sighed, and ran a hand over the front of her skirt. "It was. I'm sorry. It was dreadful of me. I just hoped...I hoped that you'd be the one to say it. That we weren't suited. To send me home and call off our engagement. That's why I told Mother and Father to be a few days behind. Not that they knew this was my plan. I made another excuse, but it was something I'd hoped for. And when I realized you were too much of a gentleman to do so, I got worried that there was nothing I could do except to do something drastic. Like last night."

"So...so we are..." He wasn't sure what to ask. What he even wanted to say.

With a gentle smile, Melanie shook her head. "I cannot marry you, Ollie. I cannot be anything more than your friend, and I hope that you'll forgive me if I've caused you any heartbreak. Please tell me you have."

Suddenly, before him stood Melanie, the girl he'd laughed with and told secrets to, the young woman who'd come to him in tears after heartbreaks, and the woman who, until the days leading up to his proposal had been his friend, and his own confidant.

Seeing her brought a piece of him back to life, even as he shook his head. "I'm sorry," he finally managed to say. "This is...this has...I am..."

Melanie reached for his hands, and squeezed gently. "My heart is full of friendship for you, nothing more. I thought that would be enough, that we could somehow manage. One day find love. But then I saw Elaine."

"Elaine?" He felt confused now, then alarm. "I assure you, I've been true. I—"

"I know you have, but you've also been dense, you silly. Yes, Elaine. She loves you, though I am not sure she realizes it, the sweet thing. And I know that I could not live with myself, denying you the person you should be with, and, simultaneously, not letting myself have a chance at a similar love, and watching her suffer."

He was unsure what to say. Elaine...loved him. Did she? He'd never imagined that. Nor this conversation. He'd felt something for Elaine, something deeper than attraction, to be sure. Had even considered it love, but he'd never allowed himself to fully explore those feelings. Not with the weight of his upcoming marriage to Melanie hanging over him.

There was a strange feeling right now. He felt lighter. Could breathe easier. When his eyes met Melanie's, there was peace on her face. It echoed in him. "But what of you?" he asked, reaching for her hand.

"What of me?" A thoughtful look grew on her face. "I don't know. Not really. But I will figure it out. What I do know, however, is that I am leaving shortly. There's no need to delay things. Don't worry," she added, holding up a hand to stop him from interrupting. "I will tell Papa and your father this was my decision entirely. I will beg forgiveness for breaking your heart. My maid will never contradict me. However, in trade, you must do something for me."

"Anything," he promised.

"Tell Elaine how you feel," Melanie said. "And, then send me a letter to let me know how it turned out."

He swallowed hard. "I don't know if I can do that."

"The post office is too far of a walk?" she asked, eyebrows raised.

"Well, not that," he protested, stammering. "The...the telling her part."

"You'd be a fool not to," Melanie told him. She released his hands, and smiled at him, shaking her head. "My Oliver, always so focused on the logical, he's not good with the emotional."

"That's true," he said with a sigh. "You know me well. But what if she gets upset? I'm her employer. I'm not supposed to love her."

"Well," Melanie said lightly, as she walked toward the hallway door, "if that were the case, many of the most wonderful and romantic stories ever written wouldn't exist, now would they? Do it so you don't live with regrets. Then, tell me so that I know my time spent here in this horribly, dreadfully boring little town wasn't wasted."

Without waiting for his answer, Melanie stepped toward the front door and opened it. He could see Lucy waiting. Their bags must have already been taken to the station. He'd been so deep in work he'd not noticed.

"Wait!" Oliver called out. He rushed over, and hugged Melanie tightly. "Thank you. I'm sorry, Melanie. I really did try."

She kissed his cheek, and smiled at him fondly. "I know you did. And now you must try once more. This time, you'll have a better outcome, I predict."

They embraced once more, and the tears in Melanie's eyes matched his own. She stepped away, went through the door, and closed it gently behind her. Oliver didn't move. Couldn't move. He hadn't expected this.

His mind reeled. Melanie was gone. The engagement was over. He was free.

Free.

The word echoed in his head, and with it came a rush of emotion so powerful it nearly brought him to his knees. Relief. Gratitude. Terror. And underneath it all, a single thought consumed everything else. He could tell Elaine how he felt.

Melanie had said it with such certainty. Could it be true? The way she looked at him, the way she'd worked through the night for him, the way she cared for him—was that love?

His heart hammered against his ribs. He needed to see her. Needed to talk to her. Needed to tell her—

But what if Melanie was wrong? What if Elaine didn't feel that way? What if he told her how he felt and she looked at him with pity, or worse, disgust? He was her employer. She depended on him for her livelihood. What if she felt trapped? Forced to say yes, just like Melanie had when he'd proposed. He couldn't do that to another woman. Not again.

Oliver pressed his hands against his face, trying to think clearly. He was exhausted. He should sleep first, gather his thoughts, plan what to say. But how could he possibly sleep now? How could he do anything but—

He started up the stairs, but the sound of a door made him stop and he called out, "Melanie?" Perhaps she'd returned. Had she forgotten something?

A moment later, Elaine appeared. "No, I'm sorry. It's just me. Did you want me to look for her?"

"No," Oliver said with a headshake. "I just wondered if she'd forgotten something." When he saw Elaine's brow scrunch, before she could ask, he said, "Melanie's gone.

She...won't be coming back. She broke our engagement." The words felt surreal saying them out loud. "We're not getting married."

Elaine looked too surprised to answer. "Are you...are you okay?" she finally asked.

"That's what I want to talk to you about," he told her.

Just then, there was a knock at the door. Quiet, timid, but a knock nonetheless.

Chapter 19

The last thing Elaine had expected to hear was that Melanie had left. A hundred questions went through her mind, all at once. She longed to ask some of them. He'd said Melanie wouldn't return. Was he sure? What had happened?

Then, there was the matter of what he wanted to talk to her about. Without Melanie here, was he dismissing her? The idea frightened her. Never mind she had been considering leaving. That would have been on her terms. With time to prepare. But now, this was sudden. Too sudden.

They both started to speak at the same time, when there was a knock at the door. Elaine turned toward it, after glancing at the clock on the wall. Too soon to be Mr. Weatherstone. Had Melanie returned?

She opened it, not expecting to see the seamstress on the other side. It was clear Oliver hadn't expected her either.

"Please, forgive me for the unexpected visit," Sally said. "It's just I couldn't continue to know what I did, and not tell you. May I speak with you?"

"This sounds serious," Oliver said from behind Elaine. "Do you want to come in?"

Sally nodded.

Elaine felt worried. Had the woman come to make a complaint about her?

"If you please," Sally said to Oliver. "I'd like to speak with Elaine alone."

"Use the sitting room," Oliver said. "I'll be in the kitchen if you need me."

Elaine led the seamstress to the sitting room, and they each sat in one of the chairs, a small table between them. Elaine observed the nervous fidgeting of the other woman and wondered why she was here.

It took several minutes before Elaine finally spoke. "I need your forgiveness."

"My forgiveness?"

"Yes," Sally said, before Elaine could ask why. "I also need you to know, what I did was for your safety, and for the love I had for my sister. I pray you grew up being cared for. It's certain, had my sister lived, you'd have suffered terribly."

"Sister? What..." Elaine stopped, shaking her head. "I'm confused. What are you saying?"

Sally moved slightly, and now she was nearly on the edge of her chair. "It's a long story. One I've kept secret for twenty-four years. I could be wrong, but I think you are my niece. My sister Elaine's daughter."

"Elaine?" she whispered. "That was the name pinned to me. I thought that it was my name."

"I could give you nothing but a chance," Sally whispered, "and your mother's name, and half my locket, so that perhaps one day, we'd find each other." She reached to her collarbone, and pulled loose a necklace. A locket.

Elaine took it from her, pressed it to her own, and the two halves fit together perfectly.

"Please," Elaine said, her throat tight with emotion as she squeezed the locket, now feeling strangely whole in her hand, "can you start from the beginning?"

"Yes." Sally nodded. Her voice quavered. "My sister fell in love with a man who was as dashing as he was kind. Our parents told her he was no good, but she refused to listen. She ran off with him, and some months later, I got a letter from her. She was desperate and afraid, and with child. In the letter, Elaine told me that she'd learned terrible things about her husband, and was scared about what might happen to her babe. She begged me to come and deliver it in secret, then hide it away, perhaps as my own, as her time was near."

"But you didn't," Elaine said. "Keep me as your own." She tried not to sound accusing, but Sally flinched just the same.

"I couldn't," Sally said, her voice catching. "Not once I was there. When I came to her to deliver you, I learned just what kind of a man her husband was. A criminal. A gambler. A man so deep in debt, he'd promised their child to someone to pay off some of it. I knew if he discovered I'd kept you, since he knew of my existence, that he'd come after me and take you anyway. What might have happened to you? It felt certain you would have been treated poorly. Hurt, even.

"The only way I could save your life was to pretend you had died and deliver you to the orphanage I'd discovered was a day away. He'd never have looked there for you. So, that's what I did. When you were born, I quickly stifled your cries. There was a medicine that, when I held it to your nose, stilled you. Made you sleep. He knew no difference between that and death. I promised to dispose of your body." Sally looked down in her lap, and tears splashed on the light blue of her dress, staining it.

Elaine's chest was so tight she could hardly breathe. Silence grew heavy.

"But what of my mother?" Elaine asked finally, longing to know yet terrified to hear. "Is she...is she..." She stopped.

"You mother. The birth was hard. She," Sally swallowed hard, and the tears turned into sobs and her shoulders shook. "I will always suspect that she took something or was given something because my sister, my beautiful older sister, my best friend, died before she could even hold you. Before she could even push you out. The only way to save you was to cut you from her."

Elaine sat back in her seat, shocked and heartbroken and filled with sorrow all at once. She couldn't imagine what Sally had gone through. Knowing her sister and her child were in danger. Having to watch her sister die, and then having to cut her open, just to save Elaine's life.

"You...you could have left me," Elaine whispered. "It would have been easier for you."

"Never!" Sally said, her voice fierce. "I promised to protect you." Some of the fire left her eyes as she whispered, "I just pray I did you no harm."

"Is the danger past?" Elaine asked, her voice low. "My father gone?"

"He is dead. A few years later, he was killed in a gunfight. It was in the papers because he was a man of some notoriety. Immediately, I went to the orphanage. You'd have been perhaps four. I tried to get you, but I had no proof of you being mine. Nothing at all. They said the locket didn't count, so they wouldn't let me take you. They wouldn't let me adopt you either. That surprised me.

Isn't that what an orphanage is for? To allow children to be adopted?"

A memory formed, hazy but real, and Elaine grasped onto it. "I remember! I remember a pretty lady in an office. I got to meet her—you—and you were crying. But you were also trying to show me something. To say something. The headmistress was talking loudly though, and I can't remember anything more."

"It's incredible that you can remember that," Sally said, her eyes widening. "I was trying to show you my locket. Tell you where I'd be. Cottonwood Falls. It's where I made a home for myself once I left you. Far enough from the orphanage not to be suspected, should anyone knowing of your existence track me down, but close enough I hoped you'd find me."

Elaine took a tight breath. "You waited all this time for me. I wasn't alone. Not really."

"Never," Sally whispered. She came over, kneeled down, and took Elaine's hands into hers. "I've thought of you every day. Prayed for your safety. And the day you walked into my store..." She shook her head. "I had no idea what to do. You look so much like my sister. I thought you were her at first. Then, when I saw the locket I hoped my prayer had finally been answered."

Elaine clung to Sally's hands. An aunt. She had an aunt. "I don't know what to say right now," she whispered. "I—"

The front door sounded.

"Mr. Waterstone," Elaine gasped, jumping up.

"I've got it," Oliver called as he passed the sitting room.

A few seconds later, she and Sally could hear Oliver greeting his client. Elaine bit her lip, unsure of what to do.

"I must open my shop," Sally said. "I know it's a lot to hear. You might have questions. You might not even want to talk to me. I'll understand that too. But come find me when you are ready. I'll be waiting. In the meantime, keep the other half of the locket. It's time it was rejoined. Like I hope we will be."

She squeezed Elaine's hands once more before dropping them and leaving the sitting room.

Frozen to the spot, Elaine watched as the woman—her aunt—walked away. Just a short time ago, she'd been considering leaving Cottonwood Falls, sure there was nothing for her here. But now, she had family. A reason to stay.

But what about Oliver?

Her mind raced back to that morning—Melanie leaving, Oliver's strange intensity, his words: *"That's what I want to talk to you about."*

What had he meant? Was he dismissing her now that Melanie was gone? Or... Her heart fluttered with a hope she didn't dare name.

She needed to speak with him. Needed to know what he'd wanted to say before Sally had interrupted. But Mr.

Waterstone was still here, and she couldn't intrude on his business meeting.

Elaine paced the sitting room, her hand clutching the locket—now whole, complete, just as she was beginning to feel whole herself. She had an aunt. She had family. But what she wanted most in the world was still uncertain.

She wanted Oliver. And she had no idea if he could ever want her too.

Chapter 20

Oliver wasn't sure who had the worst timing. The seamstress or Mr. Waterstone. How was he supposed to tell Elaine how he felt when people kept coming to the door? Worse, how could he keep his nerve up to make that confession? He found himself growing anxious and losing every bit of the courage he'd managed to pull together.

"This is good, very good," Mr. Waterstone said as he tapped his ledger, bringing Oliver's attention back to him. "Just what I needed. I'm a client for life. Send me a bill. I'm off to the bank now."

"Yes, sir. It's been a pleasure to assist you," Oliver said, rising from his seat and shaking the man's hand. He knew, had it not been for Elaine's help, the conversation might have been very different.

He showed Mr. Waterstone out, and as soon as the door closed, Elaine walked toward him, coming from the sitting room.

"How did it go?" she asked.

"I've good news!" he told her. "Mr. Waterstone is happy with the work. The work that you helped me to finish in time." Oliver hoped his voice conveyed his gratitude. And more. "I appreciate you so much, Elaine. I'm so glad to have you here."

"I am so happy it worked out," Elaine said, a smile brightening her face. Then, it turned into a hesitant look. "So, you aren't upset at me? For trying to help?"

"Upset is the furthest thing from my mind," Oliver told her. He stepped closer, and hesitantly put a hand on her arm. She didn't pull away, so he brought the other one up as well. It was dangerously close to an embrace, and he longed to step closer. To pull her near. There was a heaviness in the air. Could she sense it as well? Oliver felt the weight of all he longed to say, but the pressure of being unsure if he should.

"Elaine, I couldn't imagine being without you." He swallowed hard, wishing he wouldn't have to say what he was scared to. Hoping she'd give him a clue as to how she was feeling.

But she didn't. At least, not for a long moment, until she finally ventured, "Does this mean that you don't wish to dismiss me?"

"Dismiss you?" Oliver was sure his jaw dropped. Quickly, he said, "Why on earth would you think that?"

"Because it was Melanie who wanted a housekeeper," Elaine answered, meeting his eyes at last. "And, she has left."

"Melanie." Oliver sighed, and ran a hand through his hair. "Yes. That was...an unexpected event."

"It's quite all right, you don't have to tell me what happened," Elaine said.

"But I want to," Oliver told her, leading her into the sitting room. They sat on the small sofa together, and he told her, "She left for two reasons. The first, that she knew we shouldn't be more than friends."

"What was the second?" Elaine asked.

"You," he told her.

Her face grew stricken, and she stammered, "I didn't mean to make her leave. I'm sorry!"

"Don't be. That's not what I meant," Oliver said. "She left because she thinks that you and I would be better together."

When Elaine didn't answer, it was his turn to stammer. "I mean, not that I..." He stopped. What was he to say? How was this to continue? He felt awkward, and wished he'd never said anything. Was it too late to return to how things had been before Melanie had arrived?

Silence stretched between them, and Elaine sighed softly. "I find myself unsure what to do. I had thought that I would be leaving here."

"Because of me?" Oliver asked.

She nodded, and bit her lip. "Yes. In a way. But I've had some...news. And now I find that it, along with Melanie being gone, plus what you've just said, has me in a sort of overwhelm."

Oliver's heart hammered. Was she saying she wanted to leave? That what Melanie had told him was wrong? He needed to know. Needed to tell her. But what if—

"What did the seamstress want?" Oliver asked, curious, his words breaking in while his thoughts still tumbled around. "Was that the news? I pray it's not bad."

A small frown formed on Elaine's face, and she let her gaze drift through the window. "It was...difficult to hear, honestly. She told me a story. And how she's my aunt." She reached up to her locket, and Oliver's eyes followed her movement.

"Wait! Didn't you just have half the locket?" he asked, as his eyes fell on it.

"That's right. And now it's complete." Elaine met his eyes. "She's given me the option to go and speak with her, if I want to learn more about my mother or ask questions."

"Do you?" Oliver asked.

She was quiet for a moment. "It's a strange thing. All my life I thought I was alone, and that I had no family, and no one who cared for or loved me. It turns out that I do have someone. Someone who loved me so much, and never stopped."

"You have more than one person," Oliver said, his voice low, as his eyes blazed into her. "I...Elaine, I care for you. I love you."

A shuddering breath escaped her, and tears sprang to her eyes. "But I'm your housekeeper," she whispered. "An orphan. You're educated, from a good family, and I'm—" Her voice broke as she interrupted herself. "How can you want me?"

"Elaine." Oliver cupped her face with both hands, his thumbs brushing away her tears. "You're everything. Don't you see that? You're kind, intelligent, hardworking, honest. You see me and I see you too. Not a housekeeper. Not an orphan. The woman I love.

"I wasn't free to tell you that earlier. But, I am now. And I pray it's not too late to let you know how I feel. How I've been feeling."

Elaine pressed a hand against her cheek. "I'm not sure what to do now. I had planned to leave because I didn't think I could stay, watching Melanie and you together. I hadn't intended to fall in love with you, and I'm ashamed that I obviously hid it so poorly your fiancée recognized it. That I played a role in her leaving."

"I'm not," Oliver told her. "I'm glad she did. You didn't play a role in anything except making me realize what I really wanted. Melanie saw what I was too stubborn and too honorable to admit—that I was in love with you. That I've been miserable pretending otherwise. She told me to tell you. I…I admit. I might have kept quiet, scared to say anything without her insistence."

"But what will people say?" Elaine asked, her voice small. "I'm your employee. An orphan with no family name, no connections—"

"You have family now," Oliver interrupted. "Even if you didn't, I wouldn't care. I'll be yours, if you'll have me. We will become our own family. As for what people say," he shook his head. "I don't care. They get no say in who I will spend the rest of my life with. I'm choosing you, Elaine. If you'll choose me too."

Her eyes searched his, and she shook her head. "To think," she said, with a small laugh, "just an hour ago, I thought I was all alone in the world. Now…" She drew in a deep breath, closing her eyes as if it was overwhelming. It likely was, and Oliver's heart ached for her.

"I don't want you to feel that way," Oliver told her. "If you will have me, I won't ever leave your side."

"I would like that," Elaine said softly, looking into his face with such open affection, he felt his chest swell.

Oliver took her hands in his, holding them gently. "Elaine Winters, I know I should probably court you properly first. Take you to dinners and dances, give you time to be sure. But I've wasted so much time already pretending I didn't love you. I don't want to waste another moment. Will you marry me? As soon as we can arrange it?"

A single tear trickled down Elaine's face, and for a moment she couldn't speak. Then she nodded, laughing and crying all at once. "Yes," she whispered. "Yes, Oliver. I will."

His heart felt as though it would burst. Oliver pulled her close, and did the thing he'd longed to do for so long. Let his lips meet hers. It seemed as though all of the empty spots within him filled at once. When they separated, Elaine looked at him with something akin to amusement on her face.

"What is it?" he asked.

"I guess this means I have to move back to the boarding house until we marry," she said.

Oliver groaned. She was right. It wouldn't be proper for her to stay here, nor would it be proper if they didn't have at least a short courtship. "Shall I walk you over there, and see if she's still got your room?" he asked. "If not, I am sure Edward and Caroline have space."

"I'd appreciate that," Elaine said, and looped her arm through his.

They walked to the front door and she paused. "Before we leave, there's someone I'd like you to meet."

"Who is that?" Oliver asked.

"My aunt," Elaine said, smiling up at him. "I think it would be right if she knew of our plan as well."

"You are right," Oliver said, as he closed the door behind them. "I suppose I'd also best ask her for her blessing."

They started across the street, but Elaine slowed, her attention drawn a distance away. Oliver's eyes went to where hers were. On the town sign. He glanced at her as she rested her head on his shoulder.

"I didn't think it was true," Elaine murmured. "Though I had hoped."

"What?" he asked.

"Cottonwood Falls," she said, pointing to the sign and reading from it. "The place where dreams come true."

He couldn't answer, his heart was too full, and coming toward them hesitantly, tears in her eyes was the seamstress. Oliver watched, his own throat tight with emotion as Elaine and Sally embraced, and then reached out their hands to him.

Oliver took each woman's hand, holding it tightly. Their excited voices filled his ears, and he let himself be caught up in the moment. How could he not? Cottonwood Falls had made a promise on the sign, and his dream had certainly come true—a fresh start, a woman he loved, and a joyous future ahead—and he planned to spend every moment of the rest of his life making sure all of Elaine's dreams did as well.

Epilogue

One year later

Elaine smiled as she folded Lizzie's letter. Her friend and Mrs. Middleton, the woman who'd hired her as a traveling companion, had gotten along so well, they were still traveling. Lizzie was having the time of her life and was looking forward to their newest destination. Italy. She'd written of her desire to see the art, and had said she planned to sketch her favorites and send them to Elaine.

Soft voices trickled down the hall, muffled slightly from Oliver's study, where he and one of his clients were going over the man's ledgers.

The sound soothed her, as did the noise from the town through the open window. Elaine couldn't stop her smile.

A few days after Melanie had left, Elaine and Oliver had married. Mrs. Harper had been delighted to help with the wedding preparations, simple though they were. To Elaine's surprise, her aunt gifted her with a beautiful new dress, one of a cream silk, and she wore it happily.

Both Edward and Caroline had welcomed her into the family, and they'd spent many happy evenings together over dinner. Elaine loved both dearly, and would never cease to be amazed at how quickly she went from having no family, to more than she could imagine.

After he'd written to his parents of his wedding, Oliver's parents had visited. At first, they'd seemed strained, stiff, but had quickly fallen for the charm of Cottonwood Falls, and upon their leaving, had pleaded to be allowed to return again soon, to see their son and daughter.

Tears sprang to Elaine's eyes each time she remembered how they'd called her that.

Oliver's voice grew louder as he spoke to his client, and she looked up. The front door opened, then closed, and Oliver appeared a moment later, collapsing on the sofa next to her.

"I never imagined I'd be so busy in this little town," he admitted, running his fingers through his hair.

"I did," she told him lightly. "I've known from the start just how talented you are."

His eyes were full of love as he told her, "I've known how wonderful you were too, from the first moment I laid eyes on you."

"What do you think happened to Mr. Smith?" Elaine mused.

"I suspect," Oliver said, his voice wry, "that he got a dose in humility. A hard thing, being sent off to marry a stranger. I just hope she was kinder to him than he was to you."

"Time has softened my feelings," Elaine said. "Though I was scared, the moment I saw you, I felt safe."

Oliver kissed the top of her head, then pulled back. "Oh! I got a letter."

He pulled it from his pocket, and handed it to Elaine. She scanned it, then gasped. "How wonderful! Melanie is to be married?"

"Yes. To someone she's loved for a long time," Oliver told her. "I remember her speaking about him a few years ago. She's invited us to her wedding. If you want to go."

"I do," Elaine said. "I would like a chance to hug her, and thank her."

"Then we will," Oliver said. "I'll write her back."

He chuckled then, and Elaine frowned. "What's so funny?"

"Us," he told her. When she fixed him with a look, he explained. "We are quite a pair. You rejected the man you were to marry, and I was rejected by the woman I was to marry and somehow, it worked out perfectly, as we were suited for each other. A rejected match, you might even say."

She smiled, and reached for his hand. "Yes, I suppose we are."

There was a knock on the door, and Oliver stood. "That will be Mr. Waterstone. He's expanding, and wants me to look over this newest offer from the bank and make sure it will cover his expenses."

He brushed his lips against her cheek and left the room, answering the door. Elaine waited until he'd gone into his study, then went to the kitchen to get ready for her own guests. Her aunt, Caroline, and Mrs. Harper were coming to tea. She had some news to tell them, and hoped they'd help her figure out the best way to deliver it to Oliver.

And, she hoped Caroline and her aunt would agree to deliver the little one when it was time. There was nothing more precious than having family close by, and she knew her son or daughter would be in the best of hands—and have a life filled with love, just as its mother had.

Note from Author

Thank you for taking the time to read *Elaine's Unwanted Choice.*

Could I ask for one small favor? Reviews like yours on Amazon mean so much to me and help others to find my books! Even just a single line means a lot!

Also...

Want a FREE book?

Stop by my website to get your no strings attached **FREE book**. It's my gift to you, as a thank you for reading this one.

www.sarahlambbooks.com

Want more Rejected Books or those set in Cottonwood Falls?

You can find two more books of mine in the Rejected series!

***

Alyssa's Desperate Plan

"Yer too small on the top. I want a bigger woman."

Alyssa Moore never expected *that* to be the reason her prospective groom turned her away after one look. Now, with almost no money and no family to turn to for help, she's stuck waiting in a small town until the mail-order bride agency that sent her finds another match. She's embarrassed to seek help because that isn't her only mortifying situation, but it's all she can do.

When an upset woman finds him to ask for help posting a letter, Peter West is more than curious about her. As he learns more, he wonders...what would happen if her letter didn't post? At least for a few days. Would she consider staying there, with someone like him? He knows it's pointless. A beautiful woman like that wouldn't want a man like him.

As Alyssa becomes desperate and Peter tries to summon his courage, they'll each discover there's far more to a person than meets the eye—and that friendship and love can blossom in the most unexpected of ways.

https://www.amazon.com/Alyssas-Desperate-Rejected-Mail-Order-Brides-ebook/dp/B0CN8FKZX7

***

Joseph's Last Resort

To protect his father's ranch from a conniving cousin, Joseph McAllen has to be married before his birthday. Unfortunately, he's almost out of time. So, he does what any desperate man would. Sends off for a mail-order answer to his prayers.

Only, when she sees him, she gets right back on the stage. Joseph never imagined he'd be rejected. Filled with desperation, he reluctantly does what he should have from the start, and sends a plea for help to his aunt Rosemary. Too old and unwanted to be a bride herself, Ines Martin thought she'd be celebrating her younger sister's marriage in a few days. But when her sister elopes, scandal comes knocking and it's up to Ines to try and fix things when offered her own chance at wedded bliss—to a stranger. If she accepts, Ines sees a chance to protect her parents and make her own way. The only problem is, the man isn't interested in anything but a marriage of convenience, and Ines doesn't want to be where she's not wanted. Not one for romantic delusions, Joseph doesn't know what's worse—sophisticated and demanding Aunt Rosemary on his dusty ranch or the fact Ines might be perfect for him if he lets himself fall in love.

https://www.amazon.com/Josephs-Resort-Rejected-Mail-Order-Grooms-ebook/dp/B0DPYF9J49

***

Want to spend more time in Cottonwood Falls? You might like one of these.

***

Caroline

Caroline Watson has been living at Mrs. Hardy's School for Girls since she was orphaned. When forced into marriage by the headmistress, she plots a desperate escape the night before to the furthest place her money will take her.

Even as he tells himself he is uninterested in the beautiful brunette who appeared off the stagecoach like an angel, Dr. Edward Mason finds himself attracted to Caroline. Still, he's determined that no one is going to tempt him into a relationship ever again.

Pushed together, Edward offers Caroline a job. Just as she's comfortable and settled in, a strange man comes to town and follows her. Now she's faced with a choice. Ask for help or run again.

https://www.amazon.com/Caroline-Runaway-Brides-West-Book-ebook/dp/B0B2N32YP5

***

Rosalee

Nothing is what it seems, and she has no one she can trust.

Rosalee Milton never imagined that she'd go from a wealthy heiress to a woman in hiding, but that's just what happened. Now, she's living in a boarding house where the well meaning but nosy woman who runs the place is determined to set her up with someone. The last thing Rosalee has ever wanted is marriage, but it might be the only thing that saves her life.

Aaron Woods loathes the Milton family. He's been forced to work off a false debt by her father, and now the man demands the unthinkable. Secretly protect his daughter on a trip East. If he does, Aaron's debt will be cleared. If he fails, he'll be in jail. Getting too close might give away his true mission, but it also might be the only way to keep her safe.

Complications arise as each realizes that the very things they've been running from are no longer avoidable. Will Rosalee let herself fall in love with the man who vowed to protect her? Or will Aaron walk away, letting his feelings for her father come between them?

https://www.amazon.com/Rosalee-Boarding-Belles-Sarah-Lamb-ebook/dp/B0DXRN773F

***

Mail-Order Teacher

He thought he was heading to a teaching job, not that of a husband. Now what?

Samuel Donner, an experienced schoolteacher with a steely gaze and a firm grip on his principles, arrives in the dusty town of Cottonwood Falls answering their call for help. He's determined to bring order to chaos and transform the unruly children into well-educated citizens. His first target: the blatant disregard for attendance.

Abigail Lees, a single mother of three, struggles to keep her head above water. When Samuel visits, warning that her eldest son, Thomas, needs to attend school more often, she's surprised. Unbeknownst to her, Thomas has taken on the responsibility of providing for the family, sacrificing his education in the process.

Torn between his duty to the town and his growing affection for Abigail, and the fact another woman insists he's her mail-order husband, Samuel finds himself in a difficult position. He wants to help Thomas and Abigail, but adhering to his promise to the school board, and fending off unwanted advances, proves increasingly challenging.

Then Thomas is accused of a serious crime, and Samuel must reach a decision. Will he stand by the boy, even if it means jeopardizing his reputation and potentially betraying the trust of the community? And can his love for Abigail survive the storm of doubt and suspicion that threatens to engulf them all?

https://www.amazon.com/Mail-Order-Teacher-Honorable-Sarah-Lamb-ebook/dp/B0CQ3WZCFN

About the Author

Sarah writes captivating characters and clean romance that's anything BUT boring! From heartbreaking moments to heartwarming tales, get swept away in either historical or small town romance that pulls you in until the last page.

Nestled in the Blue Ridge Mountains of Virginia where she's married to her Texan husband, you'll find Sarah creating her next book, spending time with her children, or volunteering in her community.

Want more of Sarah's books? Find them all on Amazon!

https://www.amazon.com/stores/Sarah-Lamb/author/B098H3SGLK

www.ingramcontent.com/pod-product-compliance
Lightning Source LLC
LaVergne TN
LVHW090945080826
845145LV00003B/892

* 9 7 8 1 9 6 0 4 1 8 6 9 2 *